FINDING
DAVID CHANDLER

.A MATT HUNTER NOVEL

CHARLES AYER

"But why had he always felt so strongly the magnetic pull of home? He did not know. All that he knew was that the years flow by like water and that one day men come home again."

—Thomas Wolfe

CHAPTER ONE

DOREEN CHANDLER looked good.

Of course, Doreen has looked good to me since the moment it first dawned on me that girls looked good: a hot June day when she'd shown up at the town pool sporting this summer's body in last summer's bathing suit. She'd smiled at me.

It was June again, and hot. A lot had changed in my life since that day over a quarter-century ago. Doreen hadn't.

"Doreen," I said, stupidly, standing in the front door of the newly rented apartment I already didn't like. It was part of a complex called "Devon Wood," but the name belied the reality of the place: two acres of parking lot with red brick apartment buildings randomly erupting from the asphalt like pimples on an adolescent boy's nose. But I needed cheap, and cheap was what I got. I had signed a month-to-month lease and hoped for the best.

"So are you going to let me in?" said Doreen, hands on her hips, giving me that same smile, "or are you going to stand there staring at me like we're both still twelve?"

I should have known that she could still read my mind. She was almost forty now; we both were, but she still got away with a snugly tailored blouse and a tight pair of jeans that most women her age had quietly dropped into the Goodwill bin years ago. The couple of pounds she'd put on over the years made her look better, if anything, and I found myself wondering if the view from behind was still what it used to be. Her once shoulder length auburn hair was now short, but it was still thick and wavy, and had lost none of its rich luster. And those eyes, those witch hazel eyes, still teased me.

"Matt?"

"Oh! Sure! Come on in," I said, opening the door, wondering how long I'd been gaping. I stepped aside as she walked in and gave the place the once over. The view from behind, I was happy to confirm, was still splendid.

"You just moved in, I guess," she said, as she scanned the living room that so far I'd managed to furnish with a beat up sofa, a banged up coffee table, and a TV that wasn't plugged in.

"Wednesday," I said.

"Gee, only three days and look what you've done with the place already."

"It wasn't like I was expecting guests," I said, looking around and wondering if I could look like any more of a loser. "How did you even know where to find me?"

"This is still a small town, Matt, and in case you haven't noticed yet, you're still a pretty big name around here. It wasn't tough."

"I guess."

"You haven't changed much," she said, turning her attention to me and giving me an appraising stare like I was a Weimaraner in the Sporting group. I was wearing an old pair of khakis and a faded NYPD tee shirt that I'd snatched up off the bedroom floor and thrown on when I'd heard the doorbell ring. I hadn't shaved in two days, and I was in bad need of a shower. She was being kind.

"Neither have you, Doreen, except for the better."

She gave a quick nod of her head, as if to say that she knew that, but thanks anyway.

"So, do you think you could scare me up a cup of coffee?" she said, already heading toward the kitchen.

"Sure," I said, following her, "and I've even got cream and sugar."

"Thanks, but I drink it black now," she said, as she took a seat in one of the two scarred chairs placed around a tiny kitchen table that I'd picked up at a tag sale the day before.

"So do I," I said, as I busied myself with the coffee maker, the only appliance on an otherwise bare counter.

"Where's Marianne?" said Doreen.

"Marianne's not here," I said. Doreen knew damn well where Marianne was, and where she wasn't. She knew that Marianne wouldn't set foot in a hovel like this, and if I was living here, I was living alone. But we had to get past acknowledging the obvious.

"I gathered that from the décor. When is she going to get here?"

"She's not going to get here, Doreen."

"I hope she's all right."

"She's fine, she's just not going to be here, that's all."

"I'm sorry to hear that, Matt. Are you divorced?"

"Not yet, but it's just a matter of time. She's staying in the house in Mount Kisco with the kids. She's making all the money anyway, and she'll get the house in the divorce."

While I'd been busy deciding how best to ruin my life, Marianne had kept her nose to the grindstone, and she was now Senior Vice President of Human Resources at Allied Mutual Insurance Company, headquartered in White Plains.

"I don't mean to be nosey, but was there somebody else?"

"No. At least I don't think so. But Marianne has a lot of friends, and she doesn't like to be alone, so I'm sure there'll be someone soon."

"I'm really sorry, Matt."

"It is what it is," I said, trying to sound final. Doreen and I had grown up on the same street; we'd gone to school together from kindergarten right through high school, and she'd been my first crush. But I hadn't seen the woman in ten years, and this was all starting to get way too personal. The last year had left me rubbed raw. It wasn't like I hadn't seen it coming for a long time; but a divorce is like a death after a long illness: it still comes as a shock. Besides, there had never been any love lost between Marianne and Doreen, and I just didn't want to open up that can of worms.

"So what brings you back to Devon-on-Hudson?" she said. "Why didn't you just move to the city?"

"I don't know. I guess home is home."

"A good place to come and lick your wounds, right?"

"Maybe."

"You were gone for so long. We were starting to think you had something against the place, or maybe us."

"Ah, c'mon, Doreen."

"'Ah, c'mon,' nothing," she said. "We were all like family. We all had a great time at the ten-year reunion, and then you jilted us like an ugly date. What were we supposed to think?"

She was right. What was everybody supposed to think? But the only thing that I was thinking at the moment was that I didn't want to talk about it, at least not now, and not with Doreen, no matter how close our friendship had been. What was left of my male ego wasn't ready to have that conversation, especially with her.

Thankfully, the coffee was ready and I poured it into the only two coffee mugs I had. I gave Doreen the blue one that said, "John Jay School of Criminal Justice." I kept the commemorative "1986 New York Mets World Series Champions" one for myself. There are some things you just don't share.

"Nice of you to remember that I'm a Yankees fan," said Doreen, staring at my Mets cup.

"Even with Jeter gone?"

"Even with Jeter gone."

We sipped our coffee in silence. I was hoping it would last for a couple of minutes, but Doreen was relentless.

"I knew you'd broken up with Marianne the minute I pulled into the parking lot," she said. "Marianne doesn't love anybody enough to live in a place like this. It's not even up to your standards. How long are you planning on living here?"

Doreen had managed to insult my wife, my marriage, my admittedly modest new abode, and me, all in one breath, but I didn't let it bother me. Doreen and I had always shared the gift of bluntness.

"Long enough to decide if I'm going to stay here long enough to look for anyplace better," I said.

"Well, if you ever need help looking for someplace else, just tell me."

"Thanks," I said.

Doreen didn't reply, and this time the silence was uncomfortable.

"Look, Doreen," I finally said, "I can't tell you how great it is to catch up with you, but I feel like that's not why you came over."

"What? Aren't you happy to see me?"

"Of course I'm happy to see you. When was I ever *not* happy to see you?"

"Maybe never," she said, giving me a look that made me feel warm inside.

"But?" was all I said. The next move would have to be hers.

"But you're right," she said, after a long pause. She reached into the back pocket of her jeans and pulled out what looked like a business card. I don't think anything any bigger could have fit in there. "As nice as this has been, I didn't come over here just for a polite visit. I came here because of this," she said, handing me the card. "I found a few of these lying around in the post office so I picked one up. It's how I knew you were back, seeing as you didn't bother calling me."

I took the card from her and looked at it, although I didn't have to. It said:

C. MATTHEW HUNTER, ESQ.
PRIVATE INVESTIGATOR

It gave no phone number or address, since I hadn't had either when I'd had the cards printed up.

"So what about this?" I said, turning the card over in my hands.

"You showed up just in time, Matt," said Doreen, taking the card back like it was a souvenir and looking me straight in the eye. "It seems that you're not the only one who's been abandoned by your spouse. I figured if anybody could find out where David's gone, it would be you."

CHAPTER TWO

"**R**emember how you always got assigned to girl's Phys. Ed.?" said Doreen, staring at the card.

"Yeah, I remember," I said, trying not to wince at the memory as I poured more coffee for both of us.

My full name is Carroll Matthew Hunter. Dad had been a huge Green Bay Packers fan during their Vince Lombardi glory years, and wide receiver Carroll Dale had been one of his favorite players, a fact that played no small role in my choice of position on the Devon Central Gladiators football team. By the time I was a sophomore I was six feet tall, weighed 180, and I was fast. I could have played any position I wanted, except quarterback, of course. David Chandler had been The Quarterback in town since Pee Wee football, and he'd been penciled in as the future Devon Central varsity starting quarterback since he'd been ten years old. Besides, I knew how it would thrill Dad to see me play wide receiver, so that's what I did, always wearing Dale's number 84.

At least Dad had known that he'd saddled me with an awkward name, so I'd been called "Matt" since the day he and Mom brought me home from the hospital. Still, word gets around in a small town, and having a name like Carroll could have been a deal breaker in school if I hadn't been the co-captain of the football team.

"And what's with the "Esquire"? And when did you leave the NYPD? I thought you were a lifer."

"I thought I was the one who was supposed to be asking questions, here," I said, but Doreen wasn't having it. And she was right. A lot had happened since the last time I'd seen her, and I had some explaining to do. But not now.

"I just want to know, that's all. What, did you expect me not to ask?"

"Of course not," I said. "It's just that I don't think now's the time to get into my life story, that's all."

"I already know your life story, Matt. I was there for most of it."

"I guess you were," I said. "But look, we'll have time to talk about all that later. You came over here to talk about David, so let's get to that first, okay?"

"Yeah, okay," said Doreen, after taking a deliberate sip of her coffee, "but don't forget, I'm here for you if you ever want to talk."

"Thanks," I said, feeling grateful just to move on. "Now, what's this about David? When was the last time you saw him?"

"It was Thursday morning. Two days ago, when he left for work."

"That's not a very long time, Doreen. What's got you worried?"

"Matt, David and I have been married for 18 years, and we've never spent a night apart in all that time until the last two nights."

That sounded like David, but I had to ask the inevitable question.

"So you don't think he's left you for another woman? Your marriage was good?"

Doreen surprised me by not responding right away. She and David had started dating as high school sophomores and had been inseparable ever since as far as I knew. They had gone out on their first date a week to the day after Doreen had turned me down flat when I'd finally worked up the courage to call her up and ask her out. She'd laughed. "Oh, Matt," she'd said, "you know that you and I aren't like that." We weren't? That was news to me. I didn't leave my house for a week.

"I do not believe that he left me for another woman," she finally said.

The carefully crafted response surprised me even more, but I decided not to pursue it, at least not now.

"Have you gone to the police yet?"

"What? You mean Devon's Finest? You've heard, right?"

"Heard what?"

"Eddie Shepherd's just been named Chief of Police."

Shit, I thought.

"No, I hadn't heard that," I said, trying to sound neutral, but I wasn't going to fool Doreen.

"So what kind of help do you think I was going to get from him?"

"Have you at least called and reported David missing?"

"Yes, I did, yesterday afternoon."

"What did they say?"

"What do you think they said? They said he'd only been gone for a day and that I should call back in a week if he still hasn't come back."

"That's nothing to take personally, Doreen. If I were still a cop I would've said the same thing. The problem is they won't put out an APB or a BOLO until they're convinced he's missing."

"What's a 'bolo'?"

"Sorry. It's a 'Be On The Lookout For.'"

"Can't you get them to make an exception?"

"I doubt it," I said, "but in the meantime there's plenty of stuff that we can look into ourselves."

"Like what?" said Doreen.

"For example, have you called the credit card companies to see if there's been any recent activity?"

"I don't have to call anyone," said Doreen. "We have online accounts, and, yes, I've checked them. I handle all the family finances, so I would have noticed any irregularities."

"And you don't think he might have gotten a card in his own name without your knowing about it?"

"He could have, but he didn't."

"How do you know?"

"Because, like I said, I handle all the family finances; I have since the day we got married. I know where all the cash comes from and where all the cash goes. So if he had some secret card, he wouldn't have been able to use it without my knowledge."

"Does he have a cell phone?"

"Yes, he does, but he has literally never used it since we got it. It's on the same family plan that mine and the kids' phones are on. I see all the billings."

"Do you know where it is?"

"Yes. It's up in his bureau drawer, gathering dust. I checked yesterday morning, just to make sure. He never even bothered to charge it up. If he wanted to make a phone call, he either used the landline phone or he borrowed my cell phone."

"What about a laptop?"

"We have a laptop in our home office, but David never uses it."

"Are you sure?"

"Yes. We share an email account, and I've never seen him receive or send an email from it that wasn't just an innocent communication with friends or family, but even that's rare. When he wants to talk to someone, he calls. And frankly, I do most of the communicating for both of us."

"Are you sure he doesn't have a private email account?"

"He might," said Doreen, frowning at that one. "If he does, I know he's never used it on our family laptop."

"How do you know that?" I said.

"Because our laptop tracks all of our internet activity in the "History" function. I clear all the history once a month, but otherwise it just accumulates. So I would have noticed something like that."

I wasn't surprised. It had been the same for Marianne and me. Social arrangements, family communications, everything, had been handled by Marianne. The David I knew would have been the same.

"Does he ever get online?"

"No. I set up a Facebook account for him a couple of years ago, but he never 'friended' anyone."

"But he must've received hundreds of friend requests."

"Yes, at first he did, but he never friended back. Pretty soon, people kind of gave up."

"Does he have a laptop or a phone at work?"

"I know he has a laptop. He brings it home with him every night, and brings it to work every morning. But I've never seen him use it at home. It just sits where he drops it, just inside the front door. The last time I saw it was on Thursday morning when he left for work with it. I've never seen him with a company phone, but I guess I can't be sure." I saw the frown again. Doreen was a woman who didn't like uncertainties.

"What about his car?"

"What about it?"

"What's the make and model?" I said, grabbing a scrap of paper and a pencil from the counter."

"He drives an Audi. I think it's an A6."

"You don't know his plate number, do you?"

"For heaven's sake, no."

"What about EZ Pass?"

"David doesn't have one for his car because he never goes anywhere. Any time we take a trip, we use my car." Or, he could have wanted the EZ Pass out of his car so that he could travel with less chance of being followed, but that didn't fit the pattern based on what I was hearing from Doreen, so I didn't bring it up.

"Please keep checking the credit cards, okay?" I said, putting the scrap of paper aside.

"Sure."

It was what I would have expected. David Chandler lived a life without secrets, and he had made no attempt to establish any type of a hidden life. I'd have to keep looking, but the David Chandler I'd known all my life was simply not a furtive man, and I sincerely doubted that I'd find anything. Off the football field, he'd always been deeply shy, and that seemed to have intensified over time. But the last time I looked, shyness wasn't a crime.

"Have you talked to Kenny?" I said.

"I called him just before I came over here. He said he hadn't heard a thing. I told him, by the way, that you were back in town, and I told him where you were living. You should give him a call."

"I will."

"So, are you going to help me?"

"Of course I'll help you, Doreen." What else was I going to say? And it wasn't like I was doing anything else.

"Thanks, Matt," she said, reaching over and touching my arm, giving me another one of those heartbreaker smiles. "I knew I could count on you."

"No problem."

"Of course, I insist on paying you. Just tell me what your fees are. Do you need an advance?"

Yes, I needed an advance. And I knew Doreen could afford it. David was a vice president at the Orange County Bank and Trust, where he'd worked since he'd graduated from NYU. But no, I wasn't going to ask for one. It was a guy thing, I guess.

"We'll talk about money later, okay? I'm fine for now."

"Okay," said Doreen, "but just for now. I don't want to take advantage of our friendship." She reached over and touched my arm again.

She stood up and picked up the empty coffee cups. She brought them over to the sink, rinsed them out and left them in the sink to dry. It was only a moment, but it was the first moment that the sad little place had felt like a home to me. Some small part of me, buried deep, was suddenly content, if only for an instant.

"Now, I've got to go," she said, giving me a look like maybe she'd felt the moment, too. Or perhaps I was just imagining that. It wouldn't be the first time.

"Stay in touch, okay?" I said as I followed her back down the hallway. I didn't want the conversation to end and I didn't want her to leave, but I wasn't going to say it.

"Don't worry, I will," she replied. "And give Kenny a call, okay?"

"I'll do that right now," I said, holding up my new phone, but I knew I wouldn't. I had to ease back into this.

When she left I kept the front door open as I watched her walk to her car, a sharp looking, late model white Lexus with the top down. As she opened the door she turned to me and waved.

"Not bad, huh?" she said.

"Not bad at all."

I was pretty sure she was talking about the car. I was pretty sure I wasn't.

CHAPTER THREE

WEEKENDS IN DEVON-ON-HUDSON CAN BE SLOW, and it had been a long time since I'd been in the area, so I got up on Sunday morning and decided I'd hop in my car, a 2005 Honda Accord with a five-speed stick shift and more miles on it than I cared to think about, and reacquaint myself.

June is a beautiful time of year in the Hudson River Valley. The lush greens of the young leaves and newly planted fields hadn't yet paled under the heat of the July sun. The air felt fresh and clear, and the blue sky hadn't yet faded into its midsummer pastel. If my hard-topped Accord had only been Marianne's BMW 3-Series convertible everything would have been perfect. I opened the moon roof and made the best of it. I pulled out of the parking lot, picked a direction, and drove.

I headed over to West Point, but not to visit the United States Military Academy. The campus is beautiful, and there's a first rate museum there that I'd visited often. But today, I just wanted to see the river, so I drove up a long, winding road that was famous for its numerous accidents and even more numerous make out spots. I pulled over where there was a sign that said, "Scenic View," and got out of my car. The sign was new, but the view was timeless. This stretch of the Hudson is technically a fjord, where glaciers had carved out the valley and widened the river, leaving a spectacular vista. The Dutch had been the first settlers here, and the valley seemed to echo with the rich folklore they had left behind. I'd been away a long time, and I drank in the view the way a drunk drinks that first beer of the day.

I used to come up here a lot as a teenager, but unlike most of my friends, I never brought girls up with me. I was a star football player; I didn't need to impress girls with a view. No, I'd wanted to focus on the Valley, and I didn't want to share it. I used to stare out at the river and imagine Henry Hudson sailing upriver on his tiny ship, the *Halfmoon*, on water that looked more like a sea, smelling and tasting its saltiness, convinced that he'd found the Northwest Passage to the East Indies, the Holy Grail of early maritime exploration. I'd tried to imagine the sense of satisfaction, of pride he must have felt knowing that he'd achieved his destiny, realizing that he had done what God had placed him on this earth to do. In my young mind I imagined it was something akin to the feeling I felt after I caught yet another game-winning touchdown pass from David. And then I would try to imagine how Hudson must have felt when the water no longer tasted salty, and the river narrowed, and he had to face the crushing fact that maybe his sense of destiny had been an illusion after all. But I had always put that thought out of my mind quickly. It was a feeling I could imagine, but in my youth couldn't yet comprehend. But still, it had lingered, the *Halfmoon* never far from my mind, especially as football glory, and the youthful sense of destiny fulfilled, was replaced by professional, and personal, mediocrity.

I could have spent the morning there. The sun was shining, wispy white clouds scudded across the Delft blue sky, and the river was mesmerizing; but I had more reacquainting to do. So I got back in my car and headed back to Devon-on-Hudson, the only place I'd ever truly called home.

As I pulled in to town I slowed down to reorient myself. It didn't take long to realize that this was no longer the place where I'd grown up. Back then it was still a sleepy little village buried in the foothills of the Catskills, too far north of New York City to be a bedroom community, and too little local industry to generate any real prosperity. I'd grown up in a middle-class family in a middle-class neighborhood in a barely middle-class town with a lot of middle-class friends. Our parents drove second-hand cars; we ate a lot of ground beef and chicken, and we wore handed down clothes. It had been a nice way to grow up.

But inevitably, with the skyrocketing real estate prices in Westchester and even Rockland County, economic necessity, along with better roads, had driven people farther north. And now the slightly shabby little village of my youth was an affluent enclave for elite New York professionals. The modest house my mom and dad had bought in 1975 for $30,000 had sold for $450,000 when they'd moved to Florida two years ago. Franco's, the pizzeria in town that had served as the official high school students' hangout for decades, and which probably should have been closed down by the Board of Health, was now a trendy northern Italian trattoria called "Il Cuccina della Torino" that required not only reservations, but jackets and ties as well. It was now ostensibly owned and operated by Franco's son, Anthony, a rather slow-witted classmate who had always smelled faintly of rising dough, and who served as living proof that sometimes it's better to be lucky than to be good.

And there were the other inevitable changes along Main Street: Gray's Fine Men's Apparel, where we'd all gotten our first suits and rented our prom tuxes, was now a Verizon Store; the Tom McAn shoe store, where I'd gotten my first pair of dress shoes for twenty dollars, was now a CVS Pharmacy & Walk-In Clinic, and Ray Lutz Pontiac/Saturn on the far end of Main Street was now Ray Lutz Hyundai.

And Devon Central High School was no longer the school I had attended, which then had housed grades 7 through 12. The exploding population of the town had necessitated the construction of a new school twice the size of my alma mater, and had clearly been designed by an expensive architect who had aspired to more than simply form following function. I hated it as soon as I saw it. It had been built on the far side of what was still the football field, and my old high school was now, a freshly painted sign informed me, Devon Middle School. I decided to park my car in the far corner of the old school parking lot right off the street, where kids used to hang out and smoke, and take a walk around.

The old school looked the same, just smaller. When I'd first stepped onto the school grounds as a twelve-year old 7th Grader the place had seemed frighteningly huge. Now it seemed diminished and decidedly dowdy, especially in contrast to the new building.

Even the football field was different, I realized, as I stepped onto the gridiron. This emerald green, perfectly manicured, uniform, lush sod warming in the early summer sun but still damp with the morning dew was not the lumpy, patchy, weed-riddled surface where I'd run my routes and caught David's passes. Still, I couldn't help myself. I trotted over to the 50-yard line and lined myself up off to the right. I said, "Hut!" out loud and took off down the field on a post pattern. David was the only quarterback in the county who could throw a post pattern that deep, and I was the only receiver in the county who could get there fast enough to catch the pass. We'd run a lot of post patterns, and nobody had ever come close to stopping us. I made it to the goal line after what seemed a longer run than I remembered and made an imaginary lunge for the ball.

"Touchdown, Devon Central!" I heard a voice from behind me call out.

I spun around, and there was Kenny Cooper standing at the 30 with a big grin on his face.

******

Kenny was barely recognizable as the young man I'd last seen at our 10-year class reunion over a decade ago.

Like both David and me, Kenny was about six-one, and his playing weight had been about 190. I was still within ten pounds of my playing weight and the last time I'd seen David so was he. But Kenny had blown up. I guessed he now weighed about 260, and it was all gut. His face had grown fat and was an unhealthy shade of red, like the hamburger that looks too pink under the lights at the butcher shop. A beer tan, I think we used to call it. His hair had thinned considerably, and what was left was going to gray. He looked more like fifty than the thirty-nine I knew him to be. I tried to keep the shock off my face.

"Jesus, Kenny," I said, more out of breath than I should have been, "what are you trying to do, give me a coronary?"

"C'mon," said Kenny, walking up to me and putting me in a bear hug, "you look like you could still suit up and play. I'm the heart attack on a stick."

"How'd you know I was here?" I said.

"I didn't, but I stopped by your new place and you weren't there, so I figured you might find your way over here."

"It's sure not the field we played on."

"It sure isn't. Beautiful, huh? And speaking of beautiful, what do you think of the new school?"

"It's pretty impressive, I've got to say," I said. It was only a small lie, and I didn't want to insult Kenny if he liked it.

"Have you been inside yet?"

"No. I've only been back in town for a couple of days and, besides, I don't know if there's anyone left who would remember me."

"Yeah, we've still got a few teachers from when you and I were students, but not many. And anyway, summer vacation started last week, so it's empty now. But, hey, come with me and we can take a look. Then maybe we can sit down in my office and do a little catching up. I guess it's a little early for a beer, but I've got a fridge with soda in it," he said, with a look on his face that said he hoped that I might disagree with him about the beer.

"Yeah, I'd say 10:30 is a little early for a beer, but I could go for a soda."

"Great," he said, turning toward the school.

Kenny, probably the most bruising running back in Orange County high school football history, was a little winded just from the short walk from the football field to the school. The outside of the school didn't look any better close up than it had from a distance, but it was nice enough on the inside, at least. We wandered through unfamiliar hallways until we eventually got to a door with white, stenciled lettering on the front that said:

KENNETH R. COOPER

Athletic Director

Kenny beamed with pride as he opened the door and ushered me into what I had to admit was a pretty impressive office. At one end sat a massive desk, behind which stood an equally impressive trophy case. A spacious seating area furnished with a sofa and two chairs, upholstered with what appeared to be genuine leather, and a solid oak coffee table occupied the other end.

And in the center of the wall, between the desk and the sitting area, hung a massive reproduction of The Picture, the one that had appeared in every local newspaper in the Hudson River Valley, and had adorned the cover of our senior class yearbook: Kenny, David, and me, taken just after our final football game together as Devon Central Gladiators, helmets dangling from the fingers of our right hands, uniforms stained with grass, mud, and blood, hair matted with sweat, and our faces wearing the proud, confident smiles of youthful success. It was an image of three seventeen year-old boys on the mountaintop, seeing nothing but clear blue sky on the horizon.

We had been dubbed "The Triumvirate" by the local press, the three golden young men who, after years of mediocrity, had led the Devon Gladiators to three consecutive undefeated seasons, a perfect 30-0, culminating in the 56-0 crushing of our archrivals, the Cornwall Central Dragons. We were, quite literally, legends in our own time.

Mr. Doerr, the European History teacher, a mild, well-meaning man we used to call "Dopey," had hoped that our nickname, coupled with the school's mascot, would inspire his students to take a more active interest in the history of the Roman Empire. But when, on the final exam, he had asked, "Who were the gladiators?" and, "Name the three men who formed the Triumvirate," fully seventy-five percent of the students answered, "Our football team," and, "David Chandler, Matt Hunter, and Kenny Cooper."

"Pretty great digs, huh?" said Kenny, still beaming.

"Pretty great digs, Kenny. I'm impressed."

"You know, the head football coach reports to me, Matt. To *me*." He said it with the same immense sense of awe as if he'd said, "You know, the Pope reports to *me*."

"You've come a long way, Kenny," I said, meaning it. "Congratulations."

"There's not a single bar in this town where my money's any good, Matt. There's always a beer waiting for me before I even get a chance to ask for one. And it's the good stuff, you know, Heineken. And there's not a single event in this town that I go to, even if it's not about sports, that people don't know me as soon as I walk through the door. And you know what, Matt?"

"What, Kenny?"

"It has nothing to do with all this," he said, extending his arm and taking in his office like Hector surveying the Trojan plain. "It's still all about that," he said, pointing to The Picture. "They still remember, Matt."

"We gave people a lot of nice memories, didn't we Kenny."

"We sure did."

"We were good, weren't we."

"Damn good," said Kenny. He hesitated, but I knew what was coming next. "I still say you guys could've made the pro's."

"Aw, Kenny, it just wasn't in the cards, you know that."

"I just never understood how both of you could've just walked away from football like that, not after the careers you had here." It was a conversation we'd had many times before, usually over far too many beers, but we were apparently going to have it again. Kenny possessed the persistence of a true believer, and like a Jehovah's Witness standing at your door, it was tough to get him off the stoop.

"We played football together for a long time, didn't we?" I said.

"Since Pop Warner football when we were nine."

"And even before that. I think David's dad got him his first football when he was seven."

"Yeah, and he could always throw, couldn't he," said Kenny.

"He sure could."

"And he always threw them to you, even from the beginning."

"Yeah, he did," I said. "How many of David's passes do you think I've caught in my life, Kenny?"

"I don't know, probably thousands."

"Probably more. Nobody knew him as a passer better than I did. He had a terrific arm for a high school quarterback, the best within a hundred-mile radius of this town, that's for sure. But it would have been only a good arm at the Division I college level, and the pro scouts never would have even looked at him. And you know what else?"

"What?"

"I was a great high school receiver, but I'm not sure that I ever could have been a starter on a Division I college team, even a second-tier one, and pro cornerbacks would have chewed me up and spit me out, once they stopped laughing at me."

"At least I tried," said Kenny, his swollen jowls beginning to sag.

"Yeah, you did, Kenny, and we were all proud of you, you know that."

Kenny had gone to SUNY New Paltz for a degree in Phys. Ed., and he'd been a spot starter on the football team during his junior and senior years. He'd been a walk-on at the Jets training camp the summer after he graduated, but he hadn't lasted a week. I could still see the picture on the wall behind his desk of him in his Jets uniform. At least he had that. That fall he'd been hired as Devon's assistant football coach and he'd never left.

"And by the way," I said, looking around the office, "you've wound up doing pretty well for yourself."

"Thanks," said Kenny. "I was never brainy like you and David, but I did okay, huh?"

"More than okay," I said, thinking to myself, who was I to judge?

"So what are you doing back here in sleepy old Devon-on-Hudson? I figured you'd still be in Fun City. Aren't you Police Commissioner yet?"

"No, Kenny, I decided to leave that all behind and become a private investigator," I said, deciding to sugar coat it for the time being. My ego couldn't stand the truth right now, especially not with Kenny.

"Wow, that's a big change for you." Even Kenny sounded a little doubtful. I was either going to have to work on my delivery or just learn how to be more honest about the mess I'd made of my life.

"Anyway, believe it or not, Doreen is my first client."

"What? She told me that she'd bumped into you, but she didn't say anything about hiring you. Is this about David?"

"Yeah, it is. Has she told you how he hasn't been around for a few days?"

"Yeah, she has."

"You probably know him as well as anyone, Kenny. Are you worried? I guess it doesn't seem like the David I knew."

"It's hard for me to say, Matt," said Kenny. "It's not like the David I know either, but, you know..." He sounded hesitant, but I knew that words had never been Kenny's best friend.

"What, Kenny?"

"You know, David and me are still great friends and stuff, don't get me wrong, but I don't see him as much as I used to, you know?"

"Did something go wrong between you guys?"

"Nah, nah, nothing like that," said Kenny, perhaps a little too quickly.

"I know I haven't seen you guys in a long time, but I remember you and Allie and David and Doreen practically lived at each other's houses."

Allison Sawyer had been a cheerleader for Cornwall. I'll never forget the game during our junior year when Kenny, David, and I had jogged out to midfield for the coin toss. I remember looking at Kenny and realizing that he wasn't paying any attention to the ref. Instead, his eyes were locked on a raven-haired knockout on the other side of the field, and her eyes were locked on him. They'd had to keep it quiet until after our final game against each other, but they'd been inseparable from that day forward.

There had been an ugly rumor that Allie had had an abortion during our senior year, but Kenny had stoutly denied that it had been possible, and I'd never really believed it. What I didn't doubt, though, was that Allie Sawyer was a woman who knew what she wanted, and heaven help whoever got in her way.

"Yeah, we did. But you know how it is. The kids are getting older, and we all spend a lot of time following them around to their activities, that stuff."

"Yeah, I know the feeling," I said. "By the way, how's Kenny Junior doing? Is he mowing 'em down like his old man used to?"

"Naw," said Kenny, suddenly looking down at his shoes. "He quit football two games into last season."

"What?" I said. "Did he get hurt?"

"No. He just came to me one day and said that he didn't want to play football anymore."

"Did he say why?"

"Nope. He just said that just because I loved football didn't mean that he had to, and that he had other stuff he liked more."

"I'm sorry, Kenny, that must have been a big disappointment to you."

"I'm not gonna lie to you, Matt. I was pretty crushed."

"What's he doing instead?"

"He's playing the fucking clarinet in the fucking marching band," said Kenny, making it sound like his son had turned to hard drugs. Both my kids were in the marching band at Mount Kisco High and I was proud as hell of them, but I wasn't Kenny.

"Jesus, Kenny," I said, "I'm sorry. What did Allie think?"

"Aw, she thought it was great. The last thing she wants is for him to turn out like me."

"You can't mean that, Kenny. That doesn't sound like Allie."

Kenny gave me a look that betrayed a bitterness that I never thought I'd see in him.

"To tell you the truth, Matt, Allie and me were never like you and Marianne, or David and Doreen."

"Kenny, Marianne and I are getting divorced."

"That can't be true," said Kenny, sounding like a kid who'd just been told that there was no Santa Claus.

"I guess sometimes things just don't turn out the way we want them to." Kenny was silent.

"We can't all be like David and Doreen, can we?" I said. "They're still the golden couple, aren't they?"

"Yeah, you can say that again," said Kenny, brightening up. "Beautiful house, nice cars, great kids, David with his great job. I'm happy for them. They both deserve it."

"So what do you think is going on with David, then?"

"I don't know, Matt. But I can't believe it's any big deal. I'm thinking that David's a human being, after all, and he just needed to get away for a couple of days, that's all."

"Nothing more than that?"

"Jesus, Matt. We're talking about David Chandler here. What more could it be?"

Good question, I thought, as I got up to leave.

"It was great to see you, Matt."

"Great to see you, too, Kenny."

"Let's not be strangers, okay?"

"We won't Kenny, I promise."

He patted me on the back as I left his office, which suddenly seemed a little smaller.

I got in my car and drove back over to West Point, back to the Valley, and to the Hudson. It was a beautiful day, and I wanted to remember it that way.

CHAPTER FOUR

E DDIE SHEPHERD STOOD SIX-TWO, but he'd always been a mean little shit as far as I was concerned. Nothing had changed.

I'd started off the meeting politely enough, telling him that David still hadn't come home, and that he'd now been gone almost five days. I wanted to have a professional conversation about APBs and BOLOs.

"I always thought there was something gay about you guys," he said as he leaned back in his chair and folded his hands behind his head. His office was spacious, bright, and well furnished. The nameplate on his desk said, "Edward L. Shepherd, Chief of Police." It looked new. But it was the same old Eddie. "You know, him pitching, you catching. Is that how it was, Matt?" His smile, more like a leer, revealed crowded front teeth stained with nicotine. The small eyes and large nose completed the image of a distempered razorback.

"Still working through all those issues, are we, Eddie? I hope you're not paying that shrink too much. I'd hate to think you weren't getting your money's worth."

"Fuck you, Hunter," he said, the smile disappearing.

I knew this meeting wasn't going to be any fun, but I also knew I couldn't run away from it, so I'd gotten up on Monday morning, headed over to my office, the one with the Golden Arches out front, ate my breakfast, and checked my email using Mickey D's free Wi-Fi. The Sausage McMuffin and the coffee were excellent, and my inbox was empty. No surprises.

And so far, there had been no surprises from Eddie Shepherd.

Eddie had played linebacker on the football team, and he'd been pretty decent. He made some good plays, but nobody ever noticed him because David and I had been the other two linebackers when we were on defense. He'd also been the backup running back on offense, but Kenny had been a horse and he'd never come out of a game. Eddie had hated all of us ever since. It was all that petty.

"You just have to embrace your failures and learn from them, Eddie, that's all," I said, not exactly striving to rise above pettiness myself.

"Yeah, well from what I heard, you're the failure around here, Hunter," he said, the leer returning. "You think I don't know all about you? How you couldn't cut it with the NYPD, how you sucked as a lawyer, and how you're parading yourself around here as some kind of private investigator? By the way, I confiscated those business cards you left at the post office. I need to see your state license to make sure you're not engaging in fraudulent misrepresentation." He said the last two words like he'd just memorized them.

I pulled out my wallet, extracted my PI's license, and tossed it on Eddie's desk. While I was at it a pulled out my carry permit and tossed that over, too. He picked them both up and stared at them for a second.

"Big fucking deal," he said, throwing them back.

"So?"

"'So' what?" he said.

"The cards."

"What about them?"

"I want them back. Now."

He opened a drawer, pulled them out and tossed them on his desk. I'd only had fifty printed up and they were wrapped in a rubber band. I picked them up and slowly pulled one out. I took a pen out of my pocket, wrote my phone number and email on it and placed it carefully on his desk.

"You never know," I said.

"Yeah, right," he said. "So what do you want? I'm a busy man."

"I already told you. I want to know if you have any information that might help me locate David Chandler. His wife has hired me to look into his disappearance."

"What makes you think I know anything?" said Eddie. "It's not like Mr. and Mrs. Perfect ever had anything to do with the likes of me."

"I was thinking that since you're, you know, the Chief of Police," I said, pointing to the nameplate, "that you might be of some assistance."

"Well, I can't. Mrs. Perfect already came to me and I told her to come back in a week. Otherwise, I'd say he's off doing what a lot of men like him do: paying for what he can't get at home. Or maybe he's a closet fairy after all."

"Look, Eddie," I said, leaning forward, "I think we've pretty much established that we still hate each other's guts, okay? And I'm willing to assume that the feeling extends to David and Kenny, and to our wives. Fine. But we both have a job to do. You know David well enough to know that this just isn't like him, and I don't care if it's only been a few days. His disappearance should be regarded as suspicious, and you know it."

Eddie Shepherd looked at me with unalloyed loathing, the same way he'd been looking at me since high school. I knew he didn't want to let it go. I knew he'd crawl across the desk and try to kill me with his bare hands if he thought he could get away with it. If he had another second to think about it he just might try. On one level I understood, but on another level I just didn't give a shit. But now was the time to go with the first level.

"Eddie," I said as softly as I could, "we have to let this go, at least for now. We're both professionals. I didn't come here looking for a fight, and I don't think you want that either. You've come a long way, Eddie. You've got a lot to be proud of. Please."

"Unlike you," he said.

"Okay, fine. Unlike me."

He seemed to sag, just a little. His face seemed to relax, just a little.

"Have it your way," he said with a sigh, "but I still can't help you. David wasn't a guy who was out a lot. He didn't have any hangouts, he didn't belong to any clubs, nothing like that. It's not like anyone would miss him if he disappeared for a few days. Frankly, if Doreen hadn't come to see me I never would have known he was missing, and neither would anybody else. He was a stay at home kind of guy."

"Has he ever had any kind of legal troubles?"

"Who, Mr. Clean? Gimme a break."

"Do you know anybody in town who might have had an axe to grind with him?"

"I take it you mean present company excluded, right?"

"Yes, Eddie."

"Then no. Our hero was beloved by all. The fucking guy hasn't thrown a pass in twenty years, but he's still the Hometown Hero."

"Any theories?"

"None. Even if I gave a shit if the guy lived or died, which I don't, I wouldn't have a clue. Like I said, maybe he ran off with a woman, or even another man. You were a cop. I don't have to tell you that people can surprise you."

"You're right about that, Eddie."

"See that?" he said, the wiseguy smile returning to his face. "We can agree on something after all."

"Okay, thanks," I said. I was wasting my time here and we both knew it. I rose to leave. Eddie didn't get up from his chair.

"Hey," he said as I reached the door, "don't forget your business cards." I turned just in time to see them flying past my head. They hit the wall and fell to the floor.

"You still can't catch anything worth a shit, can you," he said, baring his yellow teeth.

I picked up the cards and left without saying another word.

CHAPTER FIVE

"I'M REALLY SORRY YOU HAD TO GO THROUGH ALL THAT," said Doreen as she placed a tray of sandwiches and a pitcher of iced tea on the wrought iron table that sat by their pool, just out of splashing range.

I'd come over ostensibly to tell Doreen about my meeting, if you could call it that, with Eddie Shepherd, but I also had another motive. One of the things I'd learned from my years as a cop, and during my failed attempt at practicing law, was that situations like this were almost always personal in one way or another; family and friends were inevitably involved. I'd known these people all my life, but I'd been away for a long time, and my conversation with Kenny had served as a reminder that I had a lot of catching up to do.

David was apparently a pretty good banker, judging from his and Doreen's home. The house itself was probably 5,000 square feet and sat on a lot that looked to be about two acres. The grounds were beautifully landscaped, and the pool area comprised not only a thirty-by-sixty foot pool, but a cabana with changing rooms, a small outdoor kitchen, a hot tub, and a sauna.

And Doreen, of course. She had mercifully donned a pair of white linen shorts when I'd arrived, but not before I'd been treated to a generous view of her derrière only technically covered by the back of her black, one-piece bathing suit. I was working very hard at keeping my eyes off her cleavage and enjoying only limited success. Doreen was doing a superlative job of pretending not to notice.

"It wasn't anything I wasn't expecting," I said, as I took a large bite out of an egg salad sandwich. I was starving. "Except, I guess I was expecting to get at least a little information out of him."

"I'm not surprised," said Doreen, taking a sip of her iced tea. She hadn't taken a sandwich for herself. "In addition to being an asshole, Eddie's a lousy cop."

"If he's such a lousy cop, how did he ever get the Chief's job?"

"I guess by kissing a lot of influential behinds," said Doreen. "And besides, this town may have grown a lot and become affluent, but the town budget hasn't grown along with it. People around here earn a lot of money, but they live expensive lifestyles, and they're not about to vote for a tax increase. The police department is understaffed, and the Chief's job only pays about half what it's worth, especially considering what it costs to live around here these days, so I don't think he had a lot of competition."

"Well, whatever, but here I am, two days into my first big private investigating job, and I've gotten nowhere so far."

"Don't be too hard on yourself, Matt. I'm married to the guy, and I don't have a clue either."

"I talked to Kenny yesterday, too," I said.

"Oh? How was he?"

"He seemed good. I wish he'd lose some weight. All that belly fat can't be good for him."

"I'm after him all the time about that, too," said Doreen, "and so is Allie, but it doesn't seem to do any good."

"Well, Kenny was never very good at impulse control. I guess people don't really change all that much."

"No, they don't," said Doreen, with a surprising amount of feeling.

"He told me that Kenny Junior had quit the football team. What was that all about?"

"That's kind of a sensitive topic, Matt."

"Why is that?"

"Take two guesses who the Devon Central starting quarterback has been for the past two years."

"I'm thinking that would be your son."

"Yes, it's Donnie. I don't have to tell you how it was."

"Let me guess: A nine year-old kid named Chandler shows up at a Pee Wee football practice one day, and from that day on, he was the anointed future Devon Central starting quarterback."

"Big surprise, right?"

"How's he doing?" I said.

"He's doing okay, I guess. The team went 5-5 last year, but they're hoping to do better this year."

"Does Donnie just have a weak team behind him?"

"Not really. It would have been better if Kenny Junior had stayed with them, but they're pretty decent."

"And you're saying that's creating an awkward situation between you and David and Kenny and Allie? You feel like Donnie would be doing better, but Kenny Junior let him down?"

"No, I'm not saying that."

"Doreen, I know you're his mother, so this is kind of a tough conversation, but how good is Donnie?"

She put down her iced tea and looked at me hard. "Let's just say that Donnie is no David, okay?"

"That must be tough for him. He has a lot of expectations to live up to."

"It's tough for all of us," said Doreen. She was quiet for a few long seconds, but I knew she had something more to say. "But that's not the really awkward part," she said, finally.

"Then what is?" I said. I was pretty sure I knew what was coming, but I didn't want to be the one to say it.

Doreen picked up her tea glass and took a sip. She put the glass down carefully.

"The reason Kenny Junior quit the football team is that he thought he should be the quarterback, and he felt he was never given a fair chance because of who Donnie's father was."

"And?"

"'And' what?"

"Was he right?"

Doreen gave me another hard look. "Maybe," she said.

"Putting aside the family stuff," I said, "that must have been a tough situation for Kenny Senior."

"I felt awful for him. What was he supposed to do, go to the head football coach, who reports to him, and ask him why his son didn't get a fair shot to be starting quarterback?"

"And what about David?"

"What was *he* supposed to do, go behind his own son's back and tell the head football coach that he might have the wrong guy leading his team?"

"That must have been terrible for the both of them, and for you and Allie, too."

"To tell you the truth, Matt, Allie and I have never been all that close. But it's been miserable for Kenny and David. Once you pulled your disappearing act, Kenny was David's best friend in the world."

"And vice versa, I suppose."

"I guess, but it was tougher on David. You know Kenny, big man around town and all that. But David's always been quieter. His life has always revolved around the kids, and he never wanted to do anything that would harm his image. So he's never been a joiner, and he kept his social life separate from his professional life. His friendship with Kenny is just about all he has."

"I'm sorry," I said, but I noticed that I'd lost Doreen's attention as she stared past my shoulder.

"And here comes the other problem," she said, quietly, followed by a louder, "Hi, hon! Come here! I want you to meet someone!"

I turned around to see seventeen year-old Doreen in a white tennis outfit striding toward us, a racket dangling from her left hand. I shook my head, and saw the real Doreen smiling at me.

"Laura, this is one of your father's and my oldest friends, Matt Hunter."

"Hi, Mister Hunter. You're the third one, right?"

"I guess you could say that," I said.

"You still look like you did in the picture."

"That's the nicest thing anybody's said to me all year," I said. Laura laughed. It was Doreen's laugh. She and Donnie were fraternal twins, I knew that much. But I hadn't seen either of them since they were barely out of diapers, so I really didn't know much else.

"So what are you up to this afternoon?" said Doreen.

"I'm gonna run upstairs and take a shower, and then I'm meeting up with Jessica and Paula. Paula's parents just got a new sailboat, and we're going to take her out for a spin on the Hudson."

"You girls be careful, do you hear me?" said Doreen. "You know how much barge traffic there is on that river these days."

"Oh, Mom, please," said Laura as she turned and headed toward the house. "Nice to meet you, Mr. Hunter." She waved her tennis racket at me.

"Nice to meet you, too, Laura," I said, but I wasn't sure she heard me.

"She may look like me, but she's all David," said Doreen, her eyes following her daughter back to the house with one of those stern maternal gazes.

"It's hard to believe they'll all be heading off to college in a year."

"It sure is," said Doreen.

"Any idea where they want to go?"

"Not really. Someplace expensive, I'm sure of that."

"They're all expensive nowadays, even the state schools."

"I just don't know how people manage. The debt kids are piling up just to get an undergraduate degree is scary, and it's just going to get worse."

"What have you told your kids about David?" I said, not wanting the conversation to jump completely off the tracks.

"I told them he got called away for business and that he'll be back soon. They aren't asking any questions for the moment, but they're smart kids, and they don't really buy it. Luckily, they're both keeping themselves busy for the summer, so they don't have a lot of time to dwell on it."

"Is Laura interested in sailing, or is she just going along to be with her friends?"

"Please. She's been winning Star Class races since she was ten. She's skippered boats all over the East Coast, and she's already making plans to sail from New York to London after she graduates from high school."

"And tennis?"

"She's competing in the Junior Nationals next month down in Florida. David is supposed to go with her."

"How do you think she'll do?"

"She's going to win."

"Wow."

"Yeah, wow."

"She sounds like a great kid. How's she doing academically?"

"Right now, she's second in her class."

"Who's ahead of her?"

"Who else? Kenny Junior, that's who else."

"What about Donnie?"

"He's in the top ten percent, but, frankly, he's not at the same level as his sister or Kenny."

"And is that what you meant when you said, 'Here comes the other problem'?"

"Not really."

"So what then?"

"She and Kenny Junior are crazy about each other. They have been since 8th Grade."

"I don't see why that should be a problem," I said.

"Neither do I," said Doreen, sighing. She looked out at the pool. I was apparently treading on sensitive ground.

"So?" I finally said.

"So Allie absolutely forbids it."

"What? Why?"

"She thinks that Kenny's never going to escape this town if he marries a local girl. At least that's what she says. She's also told him that he can only apply to out-of-state colleges, and they won't pay his tuition otherwise."

"What does she have against Devon-on-Hudson?"

"I don't know," said Doreen. "I guess you'd have to ask her. Allie's always had kind of a chip on her shoulder, but it seems to be getting worse. All I know is it's putting a lot of strain on the relationship between our two families, not to mention the relationship between her and her son. Are you finished with the sandwiches?"

The non sequitur caught me off guard for a second. "Yes, thanks," I finally said.

"I think we've had enough serious talk for one day," she said as she rose to bring the tray back into the house. "It's awfully hot. Do you want to go for a swim before you leave?"

"That sounds great," I said, "but I don't have a bathing suit."

"No problem," said Doreen, "we always keep extras in the cabana. I'm sure you can find one in there that fits you. Go change while I clean up."

In a few short minutes, we were both in the water, horsing around and splashing the way we always had. I had always been awkward in the water, but Doreen swam like a dolphin, and her sleek body mesmerized me as she cavorted around the pool.

But she wasn't Flipper. She was my client, and she was my best friend's wife.

And I was headed for trouble if I didn't keep that in mind.

CHAPTER SIX

I WAS SITTING IN MY LIVING ROOM WITH MY FEET UP eating a pizza and watching a Mets game on my newly plugged in TV. I had a half-full bottle of Budweiser in my hand and there were two empties keeping each other company in the kitchen sink. I was hoping that the combination of beer, pizza, and the Mets would help me get my mind off of David and Doreen and the whole mess for a while.

I'd been surprised to see the cable company truck parked outside my building when I'd gotten back from Doreen's. I'd been told by the customer service representative I'd spoken to, she'd actually called herself my "customer advocate," that, due to the overwhelming demand for their state of the art services, it would be at least seven to ten days before I'd be connected. The mystery was solved when, after the installation was completed, the technician, who was about my age, and whom I thought I might recognize if he took off his hat and got rid of his bushy moustache, had reached into his truck and pulled out a plastic folder that contained a page from the *Times Herald Record* dated Sunday, November 20, 1997, the day after our final victory over Cornwall. The entire top half of the page was taken up by The Picture.

"I've been waiting for this moment for twenty years," the guy said, as he lovingly removed the paper from the folder.

"For what?" I said.

"Look," was all the guy had said.

I'd seen that photo so many times that I'd stopped paying attention when I looked at it.

"I'm sorry, buddy, but I've seen this picture a lot."

"I know, but look," he said, pointing at the picture.

I looked down again, and finally saw what he'd wanted me to see: The picture been autographed by Kenny and David, but not by me.

"After you left town I didn't think I'd ever get this chance," the guy said, holding out a pen. "Please be careful, it's pretty brittle. All the acid in the newsprint, you know?"

"I know," I said, as I signed the picture and handed it back to him. He placed it back in the folder reverently, like it was an original menu from the Last Supper. "And hey," I said, pulling a ten dollar bill out of my wallet that I really couldn't afford to part with, "thanks for the prompt service."

He held is hands palms out, like I was offering him poison. "Oh, no," he said, "your money's no good with me Matt, I mean, Mr. Hunter."

"It's Matt," I said, as I gratefully re-pocketed the ten. "I'm sorry, I'm really bad with names. I know I remember you."

"It's Hugh, Hugh Bauer. Class of '98, just like you."

"Oh, yeah, that's right."

"Aw, that's okay Mr. Hunter, I mean, Matt. We were in 10th grade Geometry together. I sat right behind you, but I wouldn't expect you to remember that."

"Sure, sure," I said, not knowing what I was sure about, "good to see you, Hugh. And thanks again for the great service."

As he drove away he waved at me, a big grin on his face. I waved back. Why not?

How many more reasons did I need to convince myself that returning to my hometown was perhaps a big mistake? I'd come here to get my act together and to face the future, not dwell on past glories. I thought of Kenny, growing fat and aging badly but still stuck in The Picture, like Dorian Gray's picture in the attic, still snagging free beers off of old memories. It didn't seem to bother Kenny, or if it did he was hiding it well, but I knew I couldn't allow myself to live like that. The scary part was realizing how easy it would be if I decided to stay in Devon-on-Hudson. There were a lot of Hugh Bauers out there, just waiting for a chance to buy me a Heineken.

The game was between innings. There was still half of the pizza to deal with, and I was just getting up to get myself another beer when the doorbell rang. I felt a guilty thrill of hope that it might be Doreen, and I wished I didn't smell like beer and hadn't dropped that slice of pepperoni on my shirt. The door opened before I had a chance to get up.

It wasn't Doreen.

"What, can't you even say hello to your own sister?" said Lacey Jeanne Hunter.

"Hey, Lacey," I said, trying not to sound surprised. The "Lacey" had come from "Cagney & Lacey," Mom's favorite television show. Mom and Dad had their quirks.

She was five years my junior, but she didn't look it. Lacey had lived hard. I'll never know whether it was partly due to being forced to live in my shadow or if she was just born that way, but at the age of fourteen she'd turned rebellious in a serious way. It had started out with weed and binge drinking, but had rapidly escalated to cocaine and, finally, heroin. At the age of sixteen she'd dropped out of school and disappeared. My parents had made a half-hearted effort to look for her, but she'd worn them out, and half-hearted was about all they had left. She was gone. When they spoke of her they never sounded bitter; they spoke fondly, as of a relative who had passed away. By that time I was in New York City at John Jay getting ready to graduate and preparing for the Police Exam. I'm ashamed to say it, but I rarely gave my sister, my only sibling, much of a thought after that.

Then about five years ago she'd resurfaced. She'd looked more like forty-five than the not even thirty that she was at the time, but otherwise she'd seemed fine. She'd gotten herself clean, earned her GED and an Associates Degree in Computer Technology from Orange County Community College, and was now working for a small software firm in Newburgh. She patched it up with Mom and Dad as best she could before they'd decamped for Florida. The two of us were working at it hard, but we still had a long way to go.

Of course, we'd never really known each other in the first place, what with the age difference and my preoccupation with school and sports. I'd invited her out to Mount Kisco a couple of times, but to say that she and Marianne hadn't exactly hit it off was a gross understatement, which hadn't surprised me. By that time, if you didn't somehow further Marianne's professional goals she had no use for you, and she was petrified of what Lacey might do in the presence of polite company. At least it wasn't just me.

The one thing Lacey hadn't done, and wouldn't do, was talk about her past. She called it "The Lost Decade," and she resolutely refused to discuss it. Which was fine with me. After all those years as a cop I knew more about the lives kids like Lacey lived than I ever wanted to know, and I didn't want any of the faces that haunted my memory resembling my sister.

Still, Lacey looked great. She was rail thin, and her skin was lined, but it had good color. There was a little gray already streaking the honey colored hair that she'd inherited from Mom and still wore long; but it was thick, and it shone with good care. She was wearing a faded pair of jeans with a hole in one knee, sandals with no socks on her feet, and a loose-fitting tee shirt with a picture of Yosemite Sam on the front and the words, "Bite Me" on the back.

"Pretty swanky," was all she said as she let herself in and took a look around.

"Brave words coming from a woman who drives around in a '93 Saturn."

She glared at me. For some reason she was defensive about her car.

"Anyway," I said, getting off the subject, "it's only temporary."

"Jesus, I hope so. So you and Marianne are finished, huh?"

"It looks like it."

"Good. You don't need her brand of shit. I feel bad for the kids, though." Lacey wouldn't have been a good fit at the United Nations.

"So do I. But it wasn't exactly good for them to see us fighting all the time, and having their mother explain to them that we wouldn't be fighting if their father weren't such a failure."

"She is a sweetheart, isn't she?"

"Can I get you anything?" I said, picking up the pizza box from the table.

"Why don't you leave that pizza box right where it is and get me a diet soda. If you don't have any diet soda a glass of water will be fine."

I had a six-pack of Diet Coke keeping the beer company in the fridge, so I brought her a can and a plate for her pizza, but when I got back, she was sitting on the sofa with the box on her lap, looking completely content. She'd turned off the TV.

"The Mets suck anyway," she said.

"Thanks for coming to see me, Lace."

"I figured I might get old waiting for you to come and see me."

"I'm sorry. I've only been back for a few days and things have been pretty hectic."

"Just needling you, Matt. It's okay. So, you're setting yourself up as a private eye, is that it?"

"Yeah, at least that's what I hope to be."

"Do you have any clients yet?"

"I've got something I'm working on for an old friend," I said, and proceeded to tell her about David's disappearance.

"I've heard of these people of course," she said when I was finished. She'd polished off the rest of the pizza in the short time it had taken me to tell her about the case. "I know who Doreen is. It's hard to live in this town and not know who Doreen is, but I really don't know any of them. I remember you playing football, I guess, but that's about it. There are gaps, you know?!"

"I know," I said, "that's okay. Anyway, I'm guessing that you didn't come over to talk about my job."

"I came over here to say hello to you, of course," she said. "You're my brother and all that, but we're basically strangers, and I want to make sure we keep working to fix that."

"So do I."

"That's good to hear. But you know what? I did come over to talk to you about your job."

"What about it?" I said, afraid that she might ask me for professional help. What was it this time, I wondered?

"Don't worry," she said, reading my expression, "It's nothing about me. It's about how you're going to fail unless you let me help you."

"Gee, thanks," I said. The last thing I needed was someone to help me confirm my already prodigious self-doubts.

"Look, I'm not questioning your competence as an investigator, Matt, but being a private detective is just like anything else: It's a business. It's like being a plumber, you know? Even if you're the world's best plumber, you're bound to go broke unless you know how to run a business."

"Okay, but what makes you think I don't know how to run a business?"

"Well, first of all, I heard about your law practice."

"That's not a fair comparison," I said, but feeling the arrow hit home. "I sucked as a lawyer. It had nothing to do with my ability as a businessman."

"I heard that, too," said Lacey, with a trace of humor. She'd been through too much to waste time worrying about people's feelings.

"Thanks," I said, but I was smiling when I said it. "But then how did you conclude that I'm a lousy businessman?"

"Because, like I said, rumor had it that you'd become a private eye, so I got online before I came over."

"What were you looking for?"

"I was looking for you."

"I think you can still find me there if you Google me," I said.

"Yeah, in an old article about a trial you testified at when you were still a cop. Matt, you have no website; you're not in the online Yellow Pages; you're not even on Facebook, for God's sake. How will anybody even know to call you?"

"I guess I was kind of thinking word of mouth."

"Whose mouths? What words?"

"You probably have a point, Lace, but I don't know anything about that stuff."

"Well I do, Matt. That's why I came over. I want to help."

"But what can you do?"

"Let me get you on Yellow Pages, and let me create a website for you. In case you haven't noticed yet, big shot, you're still pretty well known around here. A decent website would be dynamite for you. I'm good at this, Matt. Let me help."

I wasn't about to say no. She spent a few minutes taking down some basic information about me.

"Good," she said. "I'll get back to you in a couple of days."

"Thanks, Lacey."

"Don't thank me yet," she said. She looked at her watch. It was a Mickey Mouse model from the Disney Store. She stood up and said, "Time to go."

"What, you don't want to watch the rest of the Mets game with me?"

"You're joking, right?" she said, but then she hesitated and her expression turned serious. "But all kidding aside, Matt, take care of yourself."

"What do you mean?"

"I just don't like the feeling I'm getting about this case you're handling for your friend."

I didn't want to ask her where she got her bad feeling, but I wasn't about to question it either. "Lace," I said, "I was an NYPD cop. I can take care of myself."

"New York City's a big place, Matt. This isn't. This is your hometown, and these are the people you grew up with. I was gone a long time, but I've been back here longer than you have, and there's something in the air that doesn't smell right about this. This could get really close to home, and I don't want you getting hurt, okay?"

"I'll be fine, don't worry," I said, but the way she was talking gave me a shiver. Lacey was clean now, but she'd survived for a long time in a very bad world on her wits and her instincts, and those antennae just don't retract. If she was concerned, that meant that I should be too. I gave her a quick kiss on the cheek.

"Okay," she said. She gave me a quick kiss back and slipped into the night.

CHAPTER SEVEN

DON'T LIKE BANKS, and I'm almost certain the feeling is mutual. We're probably both justified in our opinions.

The Orange County Bank and Trust's main branch and corporate headquarters are located in Newburgh, New York, a city with a rich past, a troubled present, and an iffy future. But like a lot of aging cities it still has good bones, including the building on Broadway, a wide avenue sloping scenically down to the Hudson River, which housed the bank. It was one of those massive piles of gray stone built in the 19th century with no consideration given to architectural grace or subtlety of style. But its stolid bearing conveyed a timeless sense of soundness, financial prudence, and permanence that more than compensated for any outward lack of refinement.

It was another perfect June morning, the bright yellow sun against the deep blue sky making the Hudson sparkle and giving the town a fresh look, like a touch of makeup on an aging woman. I walked into the building trying at least to look confident.

The interior of the building hadn't managed to withstand the depredations of time quite as resolutely as the exterior. The marble floors and the vaulted ceiling still remained, but the once magnificent open atrium on the ground floor had been divided up into small, noisy cubicles by hastily constructed particle board partitions that stripped the space of its former dignity, leaving in its place the impression that Occupy Wall Street had perhaps encamped there.

I'd called before I drove over and had been instructed to go to the second floor and turn left into the "executive suite." I had done so and was standing at the desk of the receptionist, an attractive young woman apparently named "Joanne☺." She gave me a warm smile that lingered as I gave her my card. When you've been utterly rejected by your life partner it's always nice to receive some kind of signal that you are still attractive to the opposite sex, so I gave her what I hoped was a winning smile in return.

"You look just like your picture," she said. Her reddish-brown hair was cut short and fell in ringlets around her ears, and it bounced as she talked.

"What picture?"

"You know, the big one hanging on Mr. Chandler's wall."

"Oh," I said, perhaps sounding a little crestfallen.

"I mean, you don't look as old as I thought you would," she said.

"Thank you," I said, deciding that I had no choice but to take that as a compliment. "I'm here to see the President, Mr. Martin Shoemaker. I called earlier."

"Oh, yes. Oh, I'm sorry," said Joanne, somehow managing to sound perky as she apologized.

"Is there a problem?" I said.

"No, no," said Joanne, "well, perhaps just a little one."

"And what would that be?"

"Well, you see, Mr. Shoemaker had to make an unexpected visit to another branch this morning, that's all."

"Why didn't someone call me to reschedule?"

"Well, of course, someone should have, I guess," said Joanne, her lips pursing slightly as she looked down at my card. Her hair wasn't bouncing anymore. "But, you know, I wouldn't really know. I'm just, like, the receptionist, right?"

"Right," I said. "So, do I need to reschedule?"

"Of course not, Mr. Hunter," she said, regaining some of her cheer. "Ms. Forrester, our Senior Vice President of Customer Relations has agreed to meet with you in Mr. Shoemaker's place."

"That's very kind of her," I said.

"Well, actually, it is," said Joanne. "She, like, really had to make some like, serious changes to her schedule to fit you in."

"Then I will make sure to thank her profusely when I see her."

"What? Oh."

"Perhaps you should call Ms. Forrester."

Joanne mercifully picked up the phone, and in less time than it took me to make sure I didn't have any stains on my tie, a tall, dark-haired woman in a charcoal gray pinstriped business suit over a honey-colored silk blouse came striding down the hall, walked up to me, and offered a handshake.

"Good morning, Mr. Hunter," she said, in a surprisingly high voice that nevertheless rang with authority as she shook my hand with a grip that caught me off guard. "I'm Evangeline Forrester, Senior Vice President of Customer Relations. Please call me Angie. I find it impossible to compete with the other Evangeline."

A vague memory from 12th grade English class flickered in my mind just in time for my face to assume an expression of recognition.

"Well, this isn't the forest primeval anyway, right?"

Her face lit up with surprise and admiration. It was a good face if not a beautiful one. Her nose was too large and too sharp, but her prominent cheekbones, and enormous brown eyes that emanated wit and intelligence more than made up for it. It was a face I thought I should recognize.

"Let's go to my office. I can get you a cup of coffee if you'd like, and we can talk." She headed back down the hallway. I caught up with her and walked beside her.

I'm six-one, but as we walked down the hallway I noticed that she was, if anything, a little taller than me in her low heels, and that's when it hit me.

"You're Angie Tailor," I said. "The name threw me off, but now I recognize you."

"You're full of surprises, aren't you, Mr. Hunter," said Angie.

"You're tough to forget. Between you and Rebecca Lobo, you guys redefined women's basketball. I remember you tearing it up at Newburgh Free Academy the same time I was in high school."

"Although, with you and David and Kenny Cooper sucking up all the oxygen in Orange County, I think we could've played naked and no one would have noticed."

Judging by the view from where I was standing, I think I would have noticed, but I bit my tongue. "Then you went to Cornell, right?"

"Syracuse. I went on a full basketball scholarship. But please, don't put me in the same league with Becky Lobo. I was good, but that woman was just plain awesome."

She poured coffee from a drip coffee maker into two identical blue mugs with "OCB&T" stenciled on the side in a stylized logo. "Cream or sugar?" she said.

"No thanks."

"Good, because I don't have any," she said with a grin that I liked.

I laughed.

"So am I to understand that David Chandler has gone missing?" she said, getting down to business.

"Yes," I said. "The last time his wife, Doreen, saw him was last Thursday morning when he left for work."

"That's funny," said Angie.

"Why is that?"

"Because David never came to work on Thursday morning."

"He didn't? Are you sure?"

"I'm positive, Mr. Hunter."

"Did he call in or anything?"

"Actually, he stopped by my office on Wednesday evening and said that he apologized for the short notice, but that he was going to be taking some vacation time."

"Did he say where he was going or what he was doing?"

"No. He just said he had some personal business to catch up on, and he'd probably be out about a week."

"Was that unusual for him?"

"Yes, it was. David is the kind of guy who takes the same two weeks off every summer and the same week off every spring."

"So he gets three weeks of vacation a year?"

"Four," said Angie. "He always takes the fourth week between Christmas and New Year's."

"Did you ask him what he was doing, or where he was going?"

"No, I didn't. David and I don't have that type of relationship."

"You mean you don't get along?"

"We get along just fine. It's just that David's the kind of person who keeps to himself. I never took it personally; he's like that with everybody.

Does that surprise you? You and he go way back, and people usually don't change."

"I guess I never gave it that much thought," I said, thinking about how little I had ever given anything much thought. "When David was on the football field he was an incredibly take charge guy. Always talking, always barking out the plays, always encouraging the other guys. He was kind of quiet off the field, but I always assumed that in his professional life he'd be what he was like on the field. Especially since he's a vice president and all that."

Angie paused for a few uncomfortable seconds before saying, "Not really. My impression of David is that he is a guy who wants to put in his eight hours and then get home to his wife and his kids. You have to admire that."

It was my turn to hesitate for a few uncomfortable seconds before I said, "He's good at his job, right? I mean, he'd have to be to become a vice president, right?"

"We are not unsatisfied with David's performance, Mr. Hunter, but beyond that, I'm not sure how relevant his job performance is to your investigation. David Chandler is a perfectly satisfactory employee and I can think of no job related reason for his disappearance."

Something bothered me about that comment. Something was starting to bother me about this whole conversation, but since I couldn't put my finger on anything specific, I decided to move on.

"Would it be possible to see if there's anything on his computer that might be helpful? I don't want to see any proprietary bank information. I'm just thinking that he may have sent someone an email, or someone may have emailed him with some information that may be helpful. Or maybe he keeps an electronic calendar."

"I can guarantee you that he didn't have any proprietary bank information on his computer, Mr. Hunter, but I don't have his password in any event. But we can go down to his office and take a look around if you think it might be helpful."

"That would be great. Thanks."

We left Angie's office and walked two offices down to a door that had "David M. Chandler, Vice President, Customer Relations" stenciled on it in black lettering. Angie opened the door, which wasn't locked, and walked in. I followed.

As I suspected, there was a large print of The Picture on the wall, along with other photos of his football career. There were also some photos of David smiling next to other smiling men and women who I assumed were important clients or local bigwigs.

His desk, however, was clean, with the exception of a computer monitor, a docking station and a keyboard. The docking station was empty. I guess I'd been hoping to find a note, or something jotted on a calendar, but there was nothing of the sort. I tried a drawer on his desk. It was locked, and the look that Angie gave me said, "Don't ask me to open it."

"Not much to see here, I guess," I said.

"I'm not surprised," said Angie. "David's a clean desk kind of guy. He never left his office with any clutter on it. I wish my desk looked like this."

"Did he usually take his laptop home with him?"

"I never really noticed, but I think he did; most of us do."

"So you don't see anything unusual here," I said.

"Nothing," said Angie. "This is how he left his office every night, without fail."

We left the office and walked back down the hall. On the way I noticed that the office between David's office and Angie's was occupied by "Emerson Baker, Executive Vice President, Customer Relations." Emerson was sitting at his desk, on the phone, with his feet up. I noticed that he sat up and put his feet back on the floor when he saw Angie go by.

When we got back to Angie's office I was struck by the fact that, unlike David's office, there were no photographs or memorabilia from her basketball days, only a few obligatory pictures with clients and dignitaries. I was pretty sure I spotted a picture of her with the current governor. It also struck me how much larger her office was than David's.

"Look," she said as she sat back down at her desk, "if you don't mind, please keep me up to date with your investigation. Like I said, David and I aren't close, but he's a longtime employee of the bank and he's a nice guy. I'd hate to think that he's in any kind of trouble. I'm very sorry that we can't be of more help to you."

"I most certainly will," I said, taking that as a dismissal. "And if you can think of anything that might be helpful, please contact me." I handed her one of my cards on which I had penciled in my telephone number and email address. She looked at it a little dubiously, but didn't say anything.

"I sure will," she said, giving me a friendly smile.

Joanne seemed to be busy filing a nail when I walked by her desk, and she didn't look up.

I let myself out.

CHAPTER EIGHT

WHEN I GOT BACK TO MY HOUSE Lacey was sitting at the kitchen table drinking a cup of coffee from McDonald's. There was also a cup waiting for me. She was wearing what looked like the same pair of faded jeans as the last time she was over, but this time her tee shirt said, "Red Dog Saloon, Juneau, Alaska" on the front. There were a lot of things about Lacey's life that would always be a mystery, perhaps for the best. Her eyes were focused intently on her laptop, which was open in front of her, and she looked up casually as I walked in.

"How did you get in?" I said.

"The door was unlocked," said Lacey. "Some cop."

"It's not like there's anything in here anybody would want to steal."

"You do have a point there," she said, looking around. "Even I live better than this."

"Thanks," I said, taking a sip of my coffee, which was still hot. I sat down across from her. "So, what are you doing here? I thought you'd be at work."

She gave me a look that was just about halfway between patient and condescending. "This is the twenty-first century, Matt. I work from home or wherever I want to work from. I stop by the office once or twice a week, but that's about it."

"Okay, okay. But what are you doing here?"

"I told you I'd get back to you in a couple of days, remember?"

"Yeah."

"That was a couple of days ago."

"I guess it was."

"Okay, then. Why don't you pull your chair around and I'll show you what I've got for you."

I did, and she angled her laptop so that we both could see it. She pushed a button.

"Wow," I said, as I stared at a sharp, full-color page with a header that said, "C. Matthew Hunter, Private Investigator," along with a recent photo of me that had been taken at a charity event I'd attended with Marianne, but that had been photo-shopped to look like it was a studio photo. There was also a cleverly written bio and a summary of the services I was offering. It made me sound experienced and accomplished, a true triumph of the art of fiction.

"You like?" said Lacey.

"It's terrific," I said. "Where did you get that picture?"

"I figured Marianne would post pictures of social events she thought were good for her image on Facebook, and, surprise, surprise, I was right. If you want to make any changes or additions to the stuff I wrote, feel free."

"No, no, this is great, Lace. Thanks so much."

"Now, you know what this is, right?"

"It's my web page right?"

"Right. Now, watch," she said as she exited the page, returning the search engine to her home page which was, remarkably, the Wall Street Journal online edition. Then she typed into the search bar, "Local Private Investigators," and hit the enter button. My web site came up at the top of the search list. She clicked on it and there was my new page again.

"How did you do that?" I said. "Of all the private investigators in the country, mine comes up first?"

"Only in this local area," she said. "These search engines have locator capability, so they know where you are when you make the search request. So it searched the local area just like I asked it to."

"But still, how come my site came up first? My name doesn't start with an "A," and there are a lot of other private investigators in the area."

"Because, dear brother, I gave your site a search history. It has more hits than any other investigation agency within a hundred miles."

"You could do that?"

"Yes."

"Isn't that illegal or something?"

Lacey simply stared at me.

"Sorry," I said.

"Now," she said, turning her attention back to the screen, "here you are in the Yellow Pages. I gave you a large box with your web address and email address, as well as your phone number. It'll make you stand out better."

I stared at what she'd done in less than two days, and I thought back to the week it had taken me to get those crummy business cards printed up.

"I don't know what to say, Lace. This is incredible."

"You're welcome, but now comes the hard part."

"What's that?"

"Go to your email."

I did, and in my Inbox were emails from two people I didn't know. I stared at Lacey.

"You now have potential clients, dear brother. That's the hard part."

"What do you mean?"

"You've got to do your job. I can't help you with that."

"Oh, yeah," I said, suddenly feeling in over my head.

"Oh, yeah," she said, but she was smiling.

"Hey," I said. "I hate to change the subject, but, speaking of my job, maybe there's something else you can help me with."

"Why not?" she said. "I've been ignoring my real job all morning anyway. What is it?"

I told her about my visit to Angie Forrester at the Orange County Bank and Trust.

"Sounds like it was a productive visit," said Lacey when I'd finished. "You now know that he wasn't kidnapped, which is a crucial data point. You also know, or at least can be pretty sure, that he didn't suddenly have a nervous breakdown or an attack of amnesia. He had a plan, whatever that was, and he carried it out."

I hadn't thought of any of that, but I couldn't admit that to my little sister.

"I guess that's not what I was thinking about."

"Okay, then, what?"

"Well, I always thought that when someone was called a Vice President, that meant that he was, you know, the guy second in line to the President, that he would report directly to him, you know?"

"So?"

"Well, I got the impression that David didn't report to the president of the bank, that he might have reported to Angie instead."

"Let's take a look," said Lacey, as her fingers once more started flying over the keyboard of her laptop.

"Okay," she said after a few brief seconds and again turned the screen so that I could see. "Here's the website of the Orange County Bank and Trust."

There was a large image of the bank, taken on what looked like another beautiful summer day. Above the image was the bank's logo, something that vaguely resembled a hot dog with wings with something written in Latin on the hot dog. Beneath the image was written in some kind of fancy font: *Proudly Serving Our Community For Over One-Hundred Years.*

Lacey moved her cursor over to a small box that said, "Our Management Team," and clicked on it. Up popped an organization chart. At the top was a single picture of "Martin Shoemaker, President and Chief Executive Officer." Mr. Shoemaker wore an expression that seemed to say, "Nobody calls me 'Marty.'" Beneath Shoemaker's picture were six more pictures, all of them of people with the title of "Senior Vice President." I spotted Angie's picture. It was good. She looked friendly, the kind of person you'd rather see about a loan than Martin Shoemaker. Beneath her was a picture of "Emerson Baker, Executive Vice President." He didn't have his shoes up on his desk in this image, but he had kind of a "Hi, guys!" smile on his face. And beneath Baker was a picture of David, my friend, looking somehow smaller than I'd ever seen him.

Lacey looked over and saw the befuddled expression on my face.

"Matt," she said, quietly, "there's something you have to understand about banks."

"I guess there's a lot I need to understand about banks," I said.

"Well, right now what you need to know is that almost everybody who works at a bank is a vice president."

"Apparently," I said as I stared at the org chart, which at David's level looked like the puppy section at the local animal shelter. "I don't get it."

"When people come into a bank, they want to feel like they're talking to someone important, someone with some clout; someone who's, you know, a vice president."

"So they just make everybody a vice president?"

"Not everybody, but enough to make it seem that way. If you're someone with a college degree, once you've been there a few years you're made a Junior Vice President. In a couple more years you're promoted to an Assistant Vice President, and so on."

"How do you know all this stuff?"

"Knowledge is survival, Matt. Also, the company I work for has a lot of banks for clients."

"So David's nowhere near the top of the bank's organization?"

"No, he's actually pretty far down. It sounds like that surprises you."

"It just doesn't make any sense, that's all."

"Why not, Matt? You think just because he was the quarterback of your high school football team he was destined to be the president of a bank?"

Well, yes, I thought.

"No, it's not that," I said. "It's just that David and Doreen live in one of the nicest houses in town. They're always hosting charity fundraisers and they're always the biggest donors."

"Does Doreen work?"

"No, at least not as far as I know. She always stayed home and raised the kids and managed the household."

"Did either of them ever inherit money from relatives?"

"I don't think so, Lace. They both came from families like ours."

"Then I don't get it either," said Lacey, "because a guy at that level at a local bank probably makes about $65,000 a year, and you know what that buys you around here."

"Do you think this might have something to do with why he disappeared?"

"I don't know, but it just might."

"So what do I do?"

"I know this won't be easy for you, Matt, but you might want to go and have another conversation with Doreen. I know she's an old friend, but she obviously hasn't been completely up front with you."

"Which is another reason I should be suspicious, I guess."

"Now you're catching on."

"Some private investigator, huh?"

"Don't worry about it. But Matt?"

"Yeah, Lacey?"

"Are you still sure you want to get into this?"

"What do you mean?"

"It's like I tried to tell you the other night, Matt. These people are your lifelong friends, the people you grew up with. I'm afraid you're going to find out things about them that you'd be a lot happier not knowing, that's all. Maybe you should reply to the emails you got and ask Doreen Chandler to take her business elsewhere."

"I'm not sure I can do that, Lace," I said.

"Then just be careful, okay?" said Lacey, sounding like the older sibling. "And don't forget, I'm always around."

"I won't," I said, meaning it.

CHAPTER NINE

"THAT'S THE THING I LOVE ABOUT THIS BUSINESS," said Richie Glazier, as I sat down at the far end of the bar at the Latitude Pub and Grill. "You never know what the cat's going to drag in." I hadn't been ready yet for what was going to be an awkward discussion with Doreen, so I'd wasted the afternoon learning to navigate my new website. Then I'd made myself a peanut butter and grape jelly sandwich on white bread with potato chips for dinner and washed it down with a beer. It was still early, and the Mets weren't playing, so I figured it was time to catch up with Richie.

He was a big guy with skin the color of unsweetened chocolate and a retro Afro that made him look seven feet tall. He looked great. Unlike Kenny, he hadn't gone to fat. In fact, he looked probably twenty pounds lighter than his old playing weight of 240, when he'd been a starting tackle both ways. He was also gay, which didn't bother me a bit, and I would have kept my mouth shut if it did.

"Good evening, Mr. Glazier, Sir," I said referring back to an old joke. When he used to walk up to the line before a play, Richie would look across at his usually frightened opponent and say, "If you call me Sir, I might be nice to you." Richie was never nice to anyone on the football field, but the joke carried over to his friends, and his nickname had been "Sir" all through high school.

"Good evening yourself, stranger," he said, smiling, but appraising me at the same time. "You're not looking bad for an old guy who ignores his old friends."

"You seem to be surviving pretty well yourself," I said, ignoring the jibe, "and the place looks great. Looks like you've sunk some money into it."

Richie's parents had been poor, and he'd never gone to college. Instead, he'd gotten a job tending bar and bouncing at the Latitude, which was pretty much a dive at the time. But Richie was smart despite his lack of education, and he was disciplined. After a few years he'd scraped up enough money to buy the place, which the previous owner sold to him for a song because the guy had just wanted to get out from under it, and because it was a dump.

"Yeah, I've invested in the place, but it's paid off," said Richie, scanning the crowd in both the bar and the dining room, which were both packed. Twenty years ago no one had dared order food at the Latitude, but last year a local magazine, "Hudson Valley Living," had dubbed its cuisine, "Best Pub Food In Orange County."

"Did David help you get a loan so that you could make the improvements?" I said, fishing.

"Nah," said Richie. "Even David didn't have the juice to get a loan for an uneducated black kid wanting to throw good money after bad."

I was beginning to suspect that David didn't have that kind of juice for anyone, but that was beside the point for the moment.

"So how'd you do it?" I said.

"I lived in the janitor's closet in the back till I was thirty, that's how."

"I really admire that," I said, meaning it. If I'd been that focused, maybe things would have turned out differently in my own life.

"I really appreciate your admiration, Matt," he said, "but what I'd appreciate more is a little bit of your business. You've been sitting here taking up space for five minutes now, and not even the legendary Matt Hunter gets more than that."

"You got any fancy beers that you recommend?"

"I've got some Jupiler from Belgium. Nice and light but a lot of flavor."

"Good. I'll have one."

"And would you like an order of my award winning stuffed baked potato skins to go along with it?"

"Geez, Richie, it's 9 o'clock and I already had dinner."

"And would you like an order of my award winning stuffed baked potato skins to go along with it?"

"Sounds great."

"My man."

Just as Richie was about to walk off to place my order, Kenny came through the door. He didn't just come through the door, actually. He made an entrance. He stood at the door with a 100-watt smile on his face looking like he'd just arrived on the red carpet at the Oscars. Sure enough, after only a few seconds, heads turned, followed by shouts of "Hey, Kenny!" and "My man!" He started walking toward the bar, high-fiving and shaking hands like a ballplayer who'd just hit a grand slam. By the time he got to the bar there was a Heineken waiting for him.

"Hey! Thanks Richie!" said Kenny, giving me an "I told you" look.

"My man," said Richie.

"And while you're at it, why don't you put my friend here's beer on my tab."

"No problem, my man," said Richie, as he went off to get my beer and potato skins.

"What'd I tell ya, huh?" said Kenny, giving me a friendly punch on the shoulder. From the smell of his breath, I was pretty sure that he'd already polished off his first six-pack of the evening and that his dinner had consisted of a pepperoni pizza.

"You're the man, Kenny," I said, "that's for sure."

"Damn right," he said.

And he was. Before long he was surrounded by old buddies, some of whom I remembered, and more that I should have. Some said "hi" to me, but I was now a faded memory, not one of the gang who had stayed in town, and after a few minutes Kenny and the crowd had moved off, and I was left alone at the bar with Richie.

"Does he come in here a lot?" I said, as I swallowed the last bite of potato skins. I hadn't been hungry but they'd been irresistible.

"Yeah," Richie said as he removed my plate from the bar, "probably five or six nights a week. He usually gets here after he's had his first six-pack or so at the Riverside to wash down the pizza or the foot-long sausage sub that's his usual dinner, and then he comes here for another five or six. Then he might stop off at The Clover Leaf on the other end of town for another two or three on his way home. He is, as we say, a man about town."

"And you comp him every night?"

"Yeah."

"That must be a helluva drain on your bottom line."

"Not really," he said.

"What do you mean?"

"Look, man," Richie said, starting to look a little uncomfortable, "I've already said too much."

"I'm sorry," I said, "I'm not trying to be nosy." I proceeded to tell him about David's disappearance, that Doreen had hired me to find him, and that I was just trying to gather any information that might be helpful. He gave me another appraising look.

"Okay," he said after a short pause, deciding to give me a pass on what the connection might be. "Well, the other business owners in town and I knew that we couldn't comp the guy forever, but nobody had the heart to tell him that. So I was deputized to go see Allie and have an informal chat with her."

"What, did you draw the short straw?"

"Naw, it's just that the other guys figured she might want a shoulder to cry on, and there'd be no chance of anything, you know, out of line ensuing if I went."

"'Ensuing,' huh? Pretty big word for a down lineman."

"I give my friends in the gay community all the credit for looking after my formal education. I am told that I have developed polish and excellent comportment," said Richie with a straight face.

"I bet you have," I said, looking for some signal that he was joking, but none was forthcoming. "So how did that work out?"

"Allie was upset, but I don't think she was surprised. She was more humiliated than anything, I think."

"So she agreed to pay you all?"

"Yes, and we all agreed only to charge her wholesale. We've been handling it very quietly ever since."

"And Kenny doesn't know about it?"

"Not a thing, and it's going to stay that way," he said, giving me a stern look.

I looked around the room and spotted Kenny, the center of attention, laughing and yapping, swilling yet another beer. His color was high, and he seemed to be perspiring. This was not going to end well. I finished my beer and was getting ready to settle my bill, but Richie put another bottle in front of me.

"So tell me about David," he said.

"I wish I had something to tell you, Richie."

"You must know something by now."

"Look, all I know is that he supposedly left for work last Thursday morning, and that's the last time Doreen saw him. But when I went to the bank, I was told that on the previous Wednesday evening he'd told his boss – who is not the president of the bank, by the way – that he'd be taking a few days off."

"Huh. So he's into something he doesn't want his wife to know about."

"That would be my guess."

"And here I was thinking they were Ozzie and Harriet," said Richie.

"You and everybody else," I said. Lacey's words were still buzzing in my head like a loose wire, but I didn't want to get into that right now. That would have to be between Doreen and me. "And he's also apparently not what everybody thought he was at the bank."

"Now, that surprises me," said the man I bet wasn't surprised by much. "What do you mean?"

"I mean, I thought he was one step from the president's office, but he's actually pretty far down the totem pole. And so is his salary."

"That surprises me even more. And it also makes me wonder where the lifestyle's coming from."

"Right. You got any guesses?"

"Nah," said Richie. "Doreen and I have always been tight, still are, but David and I were never what you'd call close. I think I've seen him maybe five times since we graduated. But I didn't take it personally. I think he was like that with just about everyone except you and Kenny."

"But they hosted charity galas all the time, right?"

"Yeah, but from what I could tell, that was mostly Doreen's thing. David would be there to tell his football stories for the hundredth time to anyone who wanted to hear them again, but that was about it. From what I could tell, the only things David really cared about were his kids and his reputation in the community. He's never set foot in here, and I think if you asked all the pub owners in the area, they'd tell you the same thing."

"Because he didn't want to put himself in any situations that might sully his reputation?"

"Yeah," said Richie. "You know, even after all this time, there's still plenty of women around here who wouldn't mind putting a notch for David Chandler on their belts. He didn't want to have anything to do with that, and he didn't want his kids growing up with a drinker as a father."

My gaze drifted over to Kenny.

"Right," said Richie, seeing where my eyes had gone.

"Richie, I know this is an awkward question, but David isn't gay, is he?"

"My man, that is not a question you are supposed to ask someone like me, and it is definitely not a question a guy like me is going to answer. We are a small community around these parts, and we don't rat each other out. Period."

"I'm sorry, Richie," I said, knowing he was right. There were plenty of gay cops in the NYPD, but nobody, nobody at all, talked about it.

"But he's not. No harm in telling you that."

"You're sure?"

Richie just stared at me.

"Sorry," I said again. I drained the last of my beer.

"Sounds to me like you've got more talking to do to that wife of his," said Richie, removing the bottle but not replacing it.

"I guess I do," I said, pulling out my wallet to settle the bill.

"Forget it," said Richie, holding up a giant hand palm out.

I got up to leave.

"Good to see you, man," I said.

"Same back," said Richie. "And Matt?"

"Yeah Richie?"

"Be careful, okay?"

"Careful of what?"

"You been away a long time," said Richie, "and you're getting into some heavy shit. That's all."

"Gotcha," I said, wondering how much more the man knew and wondering if it was the same as what Lacey seemed to know.

I looked over at Kenny one last time, but I don't think he noticed when I walked out the door.

CHAPTER TEN

I WAS STILL TASTING THE POTATO SKINS when I got to Doreen's house the next morning. Not that that was a bad thing.

It was already hot, and she came to the door wearing a pair of severely cutoff jeans and a "Yankees Baseball" tee shirt with, I was pretty sure, nothing on underneath. The fact that I couldn't be sure said more about Doreen than it did about me. Her hair looked hastily brushed and she wore no makeup. But she was Doreen, and she looked good.

"Matt, you're early," she said.

"Sorry, do you want me to come back a little later?"

"Of course not," she said. "Come on in."

I looked around the house with new eyes. It was clean and bright, furnished with all the right touches. The rooms were large and airy, the ceilings were high, and tasteful art hung on the walls. The air conditioning was already humming. It was easily worth three-quarters of a million, I estimated. Lacey was right: David's bank salary wouldn't even cover the property taxes on this place.

"It's already hot, so let's go and sit by the pool," she said. "I've got coffee on. Do you want anything to eat?"

"Coffee's fine," I said. I was starving, but this wasn't going to be a conversation I wanted to have over bagels and cream cheese.

She led me through the house to the door leading to the pool yard. "Go on out and make yourself comfortable; I'll be right out with the coffee."

When she came out with the coffee her hair was more carefully combed, and there was a little makeup on her face. She was still wearing the tee shirt and the cutoffs, but there was now definitely a bra underneath. I wondered if I'd been staring again.

Pool yards are nice in the morning, especially this one. It had been carefully landscaped with shrubs and flowers that sparkled with dew and shone with the vivid colors of their early summer foliage. The air was quiet, and the water was clear and undisturbed. The filter motor whispered. Birds perched on the shrubs and sang. It was a moment I didn't want to ruin.

"So, to what do I owe the pleasure?" said Doreen as she poured the coffee. Her voice sounded as sunny as the morning, but I thought I heard an undertone of tension.

"First, I'd like to apologize."

"Apologize? For what?"

"Come on, Doreen. David's been missing for a week, and I still don't have any idea where he is. Maybe you got yourself the wrong investigator." Maybe I was hoping she would agree with me. Maybe I already knew more than I wanted to know about my childhood friends.

"Matt," she said, looking me in the eye, "I still don't have any idea, either. David is an intelligent man. If he doesn't want to be found, it's going to be awfully difficult for anyone to find him. Perhaps I should be the one apologizing to you for giving you an impossible job. Just give yourself a chance, okay?"

"You're the boss, Doreen."

"Give me a break, Matt. Now, why don't you tell me what you've learned so far."

All I wanted to do was to keep things just as they were. I wanted to listen to the birds rustling in the shrubs as the dew dried. I wanted to inhale the aroma of warming grass and fresh buds. I wanted to relish that exquisite morning in the company of this warm, beautiful woman. She made the coffee taste better; she made the flowers brighter. It had been so long.

"I went over to Orange County Bank & Trust and talked to a woman named Angie Forrester," I said.

For a moment there was silence. The birds paused in mid-note. The flowers winced.

"Oh?"

"Doreen, it just isn't possible that you don't know what I found out."

"See that, Matt?" she said after a long pause while she stared at her coffee cup. "You're a pretty good investigator after all, aren't you?" She looked up at me with a smile that wasn't happy.

"Doreen..."

"Matt, it's all right. I would've been disappointed if you hadn't found out. And you have to ask about it, because you have to know if David had been involved in any shady business, or with shady people, so that we could live the way we do, right?"

"Yes, Doreen, that's right."

"And you of course assumed that I was a stay at home mom who contributed no income, right?"

"You're making it sound like I think that's something bad, Doreen. It's not like that. It's the way I thought it was, that's all."

"I know, Matt. I'm sorry. That's just the way I wanted it to look, actually."

"For David's sake?"

"Of course, for David's sake."

"Help me, Doreen. I don't get it."

"Of course you don't get it, Matt. You left. Whatever successes or failures you experienced at least weren't on display in front of a hometown crowd. But David was, you know; David Chandler, Hometown Hero, who went off to the big city to go to college and came back to marry the Homecoming Queen and become a successful banker, civic leader, and family man. He was never allowed to forget that, Matt. Never. The pressure was ridiculous."

"And I'm guessing it got even worse when he started to realize that he wasn't much of a banker."

"Well, yes and no."

I wasn't sure what to make of that answer, so I decided to let it go.

"Either way," I said, "I guess I come back to the same question: Did David get himself in trouble over money?"

"You weren't listening, Matt. No, he didn't. I took care of all that."

I didn't know what she expected me to hear, but I guessed I was about to learn.

"But how?" I said. "We grew up two houses down from each other. Your parents didn't have any more money than my parents did. Where did you get the money that would support this kind of life style?"

Doreen stared at me silently for what was, at least for me, an uncomfortably long time.

"Sometimes it's so damn tough being a woman," she said, almost under her breath as she stared at her cold coffee. "Even you, Matt. That makes it even harder."

"What do you mean?" I said, feeling myself being drawn into one of those discussions with a woman that men always lose.

"When we were growing up together, when we were going to school together, did I somehow leave you with the impression that I was stupid?"

"Of course you didn't. You were the class valedictorian, for heaven's sake."

"What a waste, right? The valedictorian should've been a boy, like David, or you, who would go on to become something more than a housewife, right?"

"Dammit all, Doreen, I never said that, and you know it. And I never thought it, either, and you know that, too."

Doreen paused for a second and then looked up at me with those eyes. I wasn't mad anymore.

"I'm sorry, Matt, I know that. It's just kind of a hot button with me, you know?"

"I know," I said, and I did. It was always a hot button with Marianne, too. It was one of the few things we agreed on. "But, so tell me. How did this all happen?" I said, looking around at the pool and the house.

"It was kind of serendipity, I guess." She put her coffee cup down and stared at the pool. "I was doing freelance software development from home. It was just after I'd had the twins, and I was doing it more to keep my sanity than anything else."

"You were doing software development? I thought you majored in psychology or something in college."

"Philosophy, Matt. I graduated with highest honors and a Phi Beta Kappa key."

"Okay. But still, it was philosophy. Where did the computer stuff come from?"

"Anyone can learn to write code, Matt. The trick is identifying a problem, thinking it through, and developing a workable solution."

"And studying philosophy did that for you?"

"Absolutely. Nothing teaches you intellectual discipline more effectively than studying the great thinkers."

"Okay, so tell me. What did you do?"

"Like I said, I was doing small freelance jobs for bigger firms. It kept me busy, and the little bit of money I earned helped pay the bills. But in my spare time I was working on something that had kind of fascinated me for a long time."

"What was that?"

"I began to think about how computers could recognize human voices."

"What did you find interesting about that?"

"Mostly I found it interesting because it was a hard problem, that's all, and because language is what separates us humans from the rest of the animal kingdom. It really engaged my mind. But I also knew that it could have practical applications. People spend a lot of time in their cars where they can't use their hands, or at least they shouldn't. And even when they're at home or at work, not very many people are good typists, and they spend a lot of valuable time hunting and pecking at their computer keyboards. So to make a long story short, by the time the twins were out of diapers, I'd developed the underlying architecture for voice recognition software. Then I patented it; and then I sold some of the intellectual property and held on to the rest for royalty income. A lot of work had to be done by a lot of other brilliant software developers over a long period of time to mature the technology and it still has a long way to go, but they all used my stuff as the foundation. Still do."

"And that got you all this?" I said, once again scanning the property.

"Oh, Matt, this is just the tip of the iceberg. I don't mean to brag, but I believe the technical term for what I made is 'a stinking shitload.'"

"So you could live a lot better if you wanted to."

"A lot better."

"But that would blow David's cover, right?"

"Now you're getting it," said Doreen, giving me one of her patented smiles.

"So you deliberately built a lifestyle consistent with the image of David Chandler, Successful Banker."

"Yes," she said, proudly. I couldn't blame her.

"And you kept all your success to yourself."

"Yes."

"Doreen, I don't know what to say. What an amazing story. I've always admired you, you know that, but…"

"Oh, stop your gushing, Matt. I like you better when the only thing you're admiring about me is my ass."

I felt myself turning bright red. I tried to say something, but all that came out was something that sounded like "gret."

"What, do you think I never noticed?" she said, laughing. "It was always one of the things I liked about you. You were just so honest about it. And after all, it's a pretty admirable ass."

"Amen to that," I said, and we both burst out laughing. I noticed the warm sun again, and the birds chirping in the thick shrubs. But I couldn't let myself enjoy it all, at least not yet. I still had another question.

"Doreen, how much does David know about all this?"

"Not much," she said, her expression turning serious again. "Just enough, I'd say."

"So all he knows is that he's making money, and you're making some money on the side, and somehow this is all working."

"Something like that. He's asked a couple of times over the years what I'm doing on my computer, but I just tell him 'software stuff' and that seems to satisfy his curiosity. He's not really very inquisitive. And frankly, David isn't all that good with money, so he's never really tried to put two and two together and make it all add up. I think he honestly believes that he still makes the lion's share, and I'm just pitching in a little small change."

"So you don't think all this has anything to do with his disappearance?"

"I just don't see how it would, Matt. Whatever he understands about our financial situation, the money has been a fact of our lives for years. Why would it have anything to do with his disappearance now?"

"I don't know, Doreen. I guess I'm just grabbing at anything at this point."

"I know. So am I."

I got up to leave.

"Well," I said, "I guess I have a lot of work to do."

"Oh, Matt, don't leave. Why don't you stay and go for a swim with me? I can make some sandwiches and some iced tea. It would be so nice."

"I really should get going," I said, with utterly no conviction.

"I'll let you look at my ass all you want," she said, with a mischievous smile on her face and the devil in her eyes. "Come on, it'll be fun."

I felt something stir that hadn't stirred in an awfully long time. I heard an inner voice warn me that this could be a big mistake. The stirring won.

"You know what?" I said, smiling back. "That sounds great after all."

CHAPTER ELEVEN

I WOKE UP THE NEXT MORNING KNOWING TWO THINGS.
The first thing I knew was that, as open as she'd been with me, and as much as I trusted her, Doreen still hadn't told me everything, not by a long shot; and I needed to know the rest of the story if I was ever going to find David. Lacey had been right. There was a lot I didn't know about Doreen.

The second thing I knew was that I was falling in love with my best friend's wife.

At least I'd succeeded in not making a fool of myself the day before, but it was more out of a fear of rejection and humiliation than any sense of honor or decency. I wanted the woman. I wanted her badly, no matter who she was married to, and there was no denying it. The stark fact, I now had to admit, was that I hadn't stopped wanting her since that day at the town pool all those years ago. I had married another woman, and I had been faithful and loving. I had gone almost a decade without seeing her. I had told myself over and over again that what I had felt for her had been a youthful crush and nothing more. But now I had to admit that I'd been kidding myself.

Marianne had always thrown that in my face when we were having fights, and I'd always indignantly denied it, but apparently she'd been right. And now I had to contemplate the possibility that my long buried feelings for Doreen had been a part of the ugly brew of misunderstandings, denials, and betrayals that had destroyed my marriage.

What made it harder was my sense that, just perhaps, my feelings were not completely unreciprocated. On the surface, everything the day before had been completely innocent. Even when we were horsing around in the pool together there had been no untoward grabbing or touching, but when she'd gotten out of the water she'd looked back at me with a grin and smacked herself on her barely concealed derrière. We'd both laughed it off, but still. Of course, I could have been imagining things. Men, especially men who have gone without affection, physical or otherwise, for as long as I had are good at that.

I also knew, while I was being honest with myself, that I should have taken that advance when she'd offered it to me on the first day.

When I'd gotten home the night before I'd gotten online and discovered my checking balance was near zero, despite the fact that I'd replenished it only a few days ago by charging my credit card. There had also been an email from the credit card company reminding me that I hadn't even made the minimum monthly payment on my balance that month, and would I kindly rectify that obviously unintentional oversight on my part? Things were starting to feel desperate.

So I got on my email the next morning and responded to one of the messages I'd received from a prospective client thanks to Lacey's efforts. It was from a man who wanted to know if his wife was cheating on him. What I should have told him was that if he was asking me, then all I'd be doing was confirming what he already knew. What I actually told him was what my rates were, and that as soon as he wired me a $500 deposit I'd get on the case. With my mind already overwhelmed with adulterous thoughts it was the last type of case I wanted, but I didn't have any other choice unless I was willing to go crawling to Doreen, and I was still too proud to do that.

Then, at lunchtime, I went over to McDonald's and got myself one of my guilty pleasures, a Filet o' Fish sandwich meal, biggie-sized. I virtuously ordered a diet soda to go along with it.

When I got back from Mickey D's there was already a reply from the guy who wanted his wife followed saying that I was hired, and that the $500 was already wired to my account. He also said his wife had told him earlier in the day that she had a last minute night out "with the girls" that night, and she'd probably be out late. He gave me his address and the make and model of her car.

I got online and made a payment on my credit card that was slightly more than the minimum, just to reassure the card company that I was a sterling customer. Then I hopped in my car and drove by the guy's address, which was in a new development built in what had been an apple orchard when I was growing up, to make sure I didn't get lost on the way over. Then I drove over to the Mid-Valley Mall in Newburgh and spent a thousand bucks on a Canon digital SLR camera with a zoom lens and all the bells and whistles. I charged it to my credit card and held my breath waiting for the transaction to clear. I tried not to look too relieved when it did. Then I went home and spent the rest of the afternoon fiddling around with the camera to make sure I knew how to use it.

I ordered a large pepperoni, mushroom, and sausage pizza around six, figuring that I needed adequate nutrition to get me through a possibly long night, and that Italian cuisine for dinner would be a healthy complement to my seafood lunch. I ate half of it and put the other half in the fridge, content in the knowledge that I didn't have to worry about what to have for breakfast the next morning.

The guy had said his wife would be leaving the house around eight, so I got in my car around seven and drove over to give myself plenty of time to find an inconspicuous place to park. The nice thing about driving a silver '05 Accord is that there are a million of them, and they attract zero attention. By seven-thirty I was tucked in about a half-block from the guy's house. I'd been tempted to stop off and get myself a cup of coffee, but I figured it would a long time between bathroom breaks, so I held off.

You would think that one of the first rules of conducting an adulterous affair would be not to drive off to a tryst in a red Mazda Miata with the top down. Apparently, however, this woman hadn't read the manual. Either that or she didn't give a shit if her husband found out. She backed out of the driveway, spun her tires, and took off down the road; I gave her about 50 yards before I started to follow her.

I'd been taught as an NYPD cop how to put a tail on someone, but my skills were wasted on this woman, who never looked in her rear-view mirror once as she zipped over to one of the older neighborhoods in town, only about a quarter-mile from my old neighborhood. She pulled into the driveway of a house that I felt like I should recognize. An automated garage door opened and she pulled in. The door went back down.

There were no shades pulled down in the front windows, but the house seemed dark. I waited five minutes for something to happen, and when nothing did I grabbed my camera and got out of my car. It was a dicey move in a neighborhood with a lot of nosey neighbors, but my curiosity was getting the better of me, and I really wanted to find out if there was anything to see in the back of the house.

I'm big, and it's tough for me to maintain a low profile, but I was familiar with the layout of the neighborhood, so I circled around to where there were some woods in the back, and then slowly crept back toward the house.

There were no lights on in the upstairs rooms, but there seemed to be some light coming from the basement windows. I crawled to within ten feet of one of the windows on my belly, careful to keep off to one side.

I got enough of a view of the basement to realize that it had been expensively refinished: recessed lighting, carpeting, an entertainment center, a wet-bar, and high-quality looking furniture.

I also got enough of a view to see a man and a woman, both completely naked, standing with their backs to me at the wet bar pouring drinks and playing grab-ass. When they'd finished pouring their drinks they turned around and headed back toward the sofa.

I tried as hard as I could to focus on their faces, but I'm a human being, after all. The woman I immediately recognized as my client's wife. She wasn't a bad looking woman and, I had to admit, she didn't have a lot to be ashamed of without her clothes on.

Oddly enough, I'd seen the man naked many times before in my life, but not in over twenty years. Time hadn't done him any favors. I also realized why I thought I should recognize the house.

The man was none other than Chief of Police Eddie Shepherd. It had been his parents' house when we were growing up, and he must have bought it or inherited it from them when they joined all the other parents in Florida.

I wasn't going to be able to stand this for long, so as soon as they put their drinks on the table and started getting down to business I picked up my camera and lined up a shot. The autofocus was fooled by the pane of glass, so I carefully focused the lens manually and waited for both their faces to be clearly visible.

The moment came, and I took my shot.

******

I was suddenly blinded as the back yard and the basement window exploded with an instantaneous burst of light from the camera's flash, which I had forgotten to take off of "Automatic" mode.

I was blinded. I heard the woman shriek, and then I heard Eddie scream, "What the fuck?!?" I heard stumbling bodies and then heavy feet pounding up the stairs.

I was just recovering my eyesight when Eddie came storming out the back door clad in nothing but a pair of boxers. His stomach hung over the waistband and his legs looked spindly, but I wasn't fooled. Eddie was a big, strong man, and he was pissed. He let out a roar that sounded like a gored bull and came charging at me. This was not going to be fun.

One of the first things I'd learned as a young NYPD patrolman about street fights is they are not fair, and the Marquis of Queensbury Rules do not apply.

So I got to my feet and kicked Eddie hard in the nuts.

He wasn't ready for it and I hit him flush. He went down hard. I was immediately on him and gave him two or three hard shots to each of his kidneys, paralyzing him with pain. I grabbed his right arm by the wrist and pulled it up hard behind him until I could feel his shoulder socket get within a millimeter of tearing.

"Eddie," I gasped, not realizing until I tried to talk how heavily I was breathing, "don't make this any worse, please. I don't want to hurt you, I really don't."

I felt him sag, and I was just beginning to think that I might have control of the situation when my client's wife came storming out the door, still stark naked, and wielding a baseball bat. Without making a sound she sprinted toward me like a hungry leopard and raised the bat. I didn't want to do this, but I had no choice. I waited until the last possible second, and then just as she began to bring the bat down, I lunged at her and hit her squarely in the solar plexus with my head. I felt and heard the air explode out of her lungs as she fell flat on her back, her chest pumping like a gaffed fish fighting for air.

I grabbed my camera and stood up, gasping. I winced as I realized that she'd missed my head with the bat, but my back had taken quite a shot. I was going to have a bruise, but I didn't think she'd cracked any ribs.

"I'll come by and see you in the morning, Eddie," I said between breaths. "Don't do anything foolish until we talk, okay?" He moaned and seemed to nod his head.

I ran back to my car, got in, and headed home. I picked up a cup of coffee on the way.

CHAPTER TWELVE

EDDIE SHEPHERD DIDN'T LOOK BAD, all things considered. He had a small scrape on his nose and a bruise on one of his cheekbones, probably from when he fell on his face, but that was about it. Judging by his expression, the deeper injuries were of a more subcutaneous nature.

I'd woken up early, showered, headed over to McDonald's for a large coffee to go, and headed straight over to Devon Police Headquarters. I pulled into the parking lot a little after seven, but it didn't surprise me that Eddie's car was already there, and when I walked into his office he looked like he'd been there a long time. The sun poured in through two large windows, and Eddie's office would have seemed almost cheery if not for the personal atmospherics.

"Here to gloat, are you?" he said, not looking up from his desk top, which was empty.

"No gloating, Eddie," I said.

"What, you're going to save it for when I get the letter from Nancy's husband's lawyer naming me as a defendant in the divorce? Or perhaps when the story gets into the newspaper and I'm forced to resign?"

"Nothing like that."

"Then what? Just to rub it in that the great Matt Hunter won again?"

"Aw, Christ, Eddie, cut it out and listen to me."

"Okay," he said, finally looking up from his desk, but still not making eye contact.

"Look, I sent my client an email last night. I told him that, yes, his wife was having an affair."

"Jesus, you couldn't wait, could you?"

"I told him," I said, ignoring him, "that that was what he'd hired me to do, and I'd done it. I didn't tell him who she was having the affair with, and I deleted the photo from my camera. It sucked anyway because of all the glare."

He finally made eye contact. "And?"

"And he fired me. Told me he wasn't going to make a final payment and he wanted his deposit back. Told me he was going to get online and trash me, put me out of business."

"So, you've decided to give up on detective work already?"

"Absolutely not. I figure the guy won't do anything because if he did, he'd have to admit that he couldn't keep his wife in his own bed. No man wants to admit that in public. I figure he'll lick his wounds and go away. So, your only concern is your friend Nancy. Maybe you ought to call her and tell her to keep her mouth shut."

"Thanks for the advice. You finished?"

"No."

"Okay. What then?"

"David Chandler."

"Ah, yes. Saint David of Devon. You're telling me he hasn't turned up yet?"

"No, he hasn't."

"Gee, that's a shame. Princess Doreen must be distraught."

"As a matter of fact, she is."

"Is this the part where I'm supposed to tell you I give a fuck?" said Eddie, the familiar sneer returning to his face. "The part where I should be falling down on my knees and thanking you for doing me a favor and gratefully offering to do anything you ask in return?"

"No, Eddie," I said, working hard to keep my voice neutral.

"Then I don't get it."

I didn't get it either, but I wasn't going to tell him that. I still hated the guy. I should have been savoring the opportunity to nail his crummy hide to the wall, but it just wasn't happening. I'd have to think about that later.

"It's the part where you're supposed to do your job and work with me to find him," I said. He just stared back at me, so I said, "Look, Eddie, with any luck I'm going to be around for a long time, and so are you. Whatever went on that made us hate each other happened a lifetime ago. I'm not asking you to like me; hell, I'm not even asking myself to like you. I'm just saying that we ought to let go of the grudges at least enough to work together, especially when a guy's life might be at stake."

Eddie was silent for a long time. He looked back down at his desk. The bruise on his cheek seemed to redden. He took a deep breath and exhaled.

"Okay," he said, still not looking at me. "What do you want?"

"I want you to file a missing person report. I also want to you send out an All Points Bulletin with the make, model and tag numbers of his car. I want you to send out a Be On The Lookout bulletin with his name, his photo, and a description."

Another pause. "Okay," he said, finally, "I'll get to it as soon as I can. I've got other things to do around here, you know."

I pulled out a sheaf of papers that I'd brought with me in a manila folder.

"Here," I said. "I did it all for you, figuring you'd be busy." It was all stuff I'd done a million times as a cop. It had only taken me a few minutes and it was perfect. All Eddie had to do was get his secretary to copy it off on official letterhead and fax it out.

He stared at the paperwork for a long time.

"Okay," he said, still not looking at me, "I'll get it out this morning."

"Thanks, Eddie," I said, trying to sound like I meant it. I got up to leave. "I'll give you a call if I find anything more out."

"Okay," he said, and then he surprised me by saying, "I'll do the same."

I headed for the door.

"And Matt?" I heard him say from behind me. I turned back toward him.

"Yeah, Eddie?"

He sat there a long time, staring at me. Then he turned his gaze back to the sheaf of papers on his desk.

"Nothing," he finally said.

It was the nicest thing he'd said to me since junior high. I turned back and walked out the door.

Outside, it was another perfect summer day. The air was cool, but the morning sun warmed my skin. I got in my car, rolled down the windows, and pulled out of the parking lot, hearing the gravel on the pavement crunch under my tires. I wanted to drive over to Doreen's and tell her all about it, but that was an impulse I had to resist, at least for a couple of hours.

It was still early and I was hungry. I swung by McDonald's and bought another cup of coffee, then I went home and finished the pizza.

CHAPTER THIRTEEN

D OREEN MADE THINGS EASY FOR ME by calling me up a little before lunchtime and asking me to stop by. She didn't give me an explanation, but I didn't need one. I hopped in my car and headed over. I wondered if my bathing suit was dry.

But when I got there she greeted me at the door wearing a pair of rust colored linen slacks and a white cotton blouse. She escorted me into the kitchen. She gestured toward the large, round table that dominated the center of the room and said, "Why don't you sit down while I pour us some coffee."

"Is everything okay?" I said, taking a seat.

"Of course everything isn't okay, Matt."

"I'm sorry, that was stupid."

"Forget about it," she said as she filled two steaming mugs and brought them over to the table.

"Sure," I said. "So what's up? Have you heard anything?"

"No, I haven't," she said, as she raised her cup to her lips. I couldn't help noticing that her hand shook a little and her movements had a stiffness to them that I hadn't seen before.

"I don't mean to be pushy," I said, "but it seemed like you asked me to come over for a reason."

She put her cup down on the table and rested her forehead against the palm of her left hand. She was silent for a few minutes, but I waited.

"Maybe I just need someone to talk to," she finally said, her forehead still resting on her hand.

"Maybe," I said, not believing it. "Is this about your kids? They're both too smart to stay quiet about this for too much longer."

"Funny you should ask," she said, finally lifting her head and taking a sip of her coffee. "They're both awfully busy, and we don't see that much of each other, so I've been able to dodge the issue without being too obvious about it. But last night we were all home for dinner and they kind of ambushed me."

"What did you say?"

"I told them the truth. That's what I always do with my kids. They're too smart to fool, so why try?"

"Kind of like their mother," I said. That got a little laugh out of her, but it didn't sound happy. How much did you tell them?"

"I told them what I knew, which wasn't much, of course."

"Did you ask them if they'd noticed anything odd about their father's behavior recently?"

"As a matter of fact I did, but they both came up empty. He'd been just the same old Dad as far as they could tell."

"That's what kids want to see, I guess."

"You're probably right, but I had to ask."

"How are they handling it all?"

"You know kids," said Doreen. "They tried to act like they were dealing with it, but I know they're both really upset."

"Doreen," I said, after a brief, uncomfortable silence, "are you sure there isn't something else you wanted to talk to me about?"

She sat still for a moment, then drained her coffee cup and stood up.

"I want to go for a swim," she said. "Your bathing suit's hanging in the cabana. I'll be right down."

It wasn't a suggestion, so there wasn't much sense in arguing. Anyway, I didn't want to.

By the time Doreen got back I'd changed and was lying face down on one of the half-dozen or so *chaises longues* situated around the perimeter of the pool. When I looked up I noticed that she was wearing a different suit, one that was more conservatively cut in the crucial areas. I didn't know whether to feel relieved or disappointed. Yes I did.

"Jesus, Matt, what happened?" she said, staring down at my back, an appalled expression on her face.

"What do you mean?"

"I mean you've got a bruise covering half your back."

"I do?" I said. I only had one small mirror in my house and I hadn't bothered to try to look.

"You certainly do," she said, sitting down beside me on the chaise. "It must hurt like hell. So tell me, what happened?"

I started to tell her of my previous night's adventures, which she probably needed to know anyway. While I was talking she started gently running her hands over the bruised area of my back. Maybe it was nothing more than a professional masseuse would have done, but by the time I'd finished my story she had me so thoroughly aroused that I couldn't have turned over if I'd wanted to.

"Anyway," I said, trying to keep my mind focused, "at least it gave me some leverage with the guy." I proceeded to tell her about my morning meeting.

"I'm proud of you, Matt," she said, when I was done.

"What, for doing my job badly?"

"Don't be an idiot," she said, her fingers penetrating more deeply into my back. "I meant for the way you handled Eddie. That took a lot of guts."

"I was just trying to be practical about it, that's all."

"Maybe, but it was also an utterly decent thing to do."

"Anyway, I'm sorry this is taking so long, but, personal issues aside, we just weren't going to get any traction with the police until a week had passed, and I'm sorry about that. Hopefully, we'll start making some progress now."

I finally had an opportunity to move, so I rolled over and sat up. Doreen sat down beside me.

"I still haven't told you why I asked you over, have I?" she said.

"No, you haven't."

"It's an awkward discussion, Matt, and I don't even know if it's related to David's disappearance, which is why I haven't brought it up until now."

"But now David's been gone a week."

"Yes. I guess I just didn't believe it would go on for this long."

"Neither did I, but here we are. So, what is it?"

"I'm not sure I know where to start," she said.

"How about at the beginning?" I said, trying not to sound impatient.

"Good idea," she said, smiling at me, "but let me get us some iced tea first."

"Okay," I said. She was buying time and we both knew it, but I had to let her do this her way; and, besides, it wasn't like I was going anywhere.

When Doreen got back she surprised me by sitting back down next to me on the *chaise longue* instead of inviting me over to sit at a table. Our thighs were touching. I thought she'd resettle herself and create some space, but she didn't. I certainly didn't.

"Okay," she said, taking a sip of tea. "This starts a long time ago. I don't remember exactly when, but the kids were really little."

"So, maybe fifteen years ago?"

"That sounds about right. Anyway, I remember one night, just after we'd gotten the kids to bed, David asked me to come into the living room and sit down because we had to talk about something."

"That must have sounded ominous."

"Yeah, it did, but it was nothing that I was afraid it might be."

"What, were you afraid that he was going to ask you for a divorce or something?"

"No, of course not," she said dismissively. "I thought maybe someone had died or was really sick or something."

"But it wasn't that."

"No."

"Then what?"

"He told me that Allie Cooper had come to see him at the bank that afternoon. She said she had to talk to him about Kenny."

"Was he already drinking too much?"

"I don't know, but that's not what she needed to talk to David about. She said she needed some money."

"Money? How much?"

"Two thousand dollars."

"Ouch," I said. "That doesn't sound like a lot now, but back then, and given what we were all making, that was a pretty serious request."

"You're right, it was. But by that time I'd already sold my first patent so I wasn't worried about the money."

"So, did she explain what she needed it for?"

"David told me that she said that they'd gotten themselves in over their heads with the house and cars they'd bought. She said that Kenny wasn't good with money, and he'd made some rash purchases. She also said that she'd taken over the finances now, and that this would just be a one-time favor."

"And David didn't want to part with that much money, even for a friend, without talking to you about it."

"I handled all the family finances, and on top of that, he didn't have any idea how much money that one patent sale had raked in, so he didn't know if we could afford it."

"So David never even handled the family checkbook?"

"I wouldn't let him near it; he was helpless. Between him and Kenny they couldn't have run a lemonade stand without losing track of the dimes."

"So you paid it."

"Yes."

"And that was it?"

"Yeah, for about a year, and then the same thing happened. She made all the same promises, but this time she asked for three thousand dollars. And the year after that, and the year after that. After three or four years the amount was up to ten-thousand dollars, and the requests were coming every six months."

"And you kept paying it?"

"It was Kenny, Matt, and it wasn't like I couldn't afford it."

"Did Allie give Matt any explanations?"

"Not directly, but she kind of hinted that not only was Kenny drinking most of his paycheck, but he'd also gotten into some gambling problems."

"Shit. I hate to say it, but it sounds like Kenny. He was always just one great, big, uncontrollable impulse."

"Yeah, that's Kenny," said Doreen. Somehow her hand had settled on my thigh.

"So, is this still going on?"

"That's what we need to talk about, Matt. No, it's not."

"What happened?" I asked.

"A couple of months ago David came to me and said that this time Allie had asked for $150,000. It had never been more than $20,000 before that."

"What did you do?"

"I hit the roof. I said no."

"That was too much even for you, huh?"

"I could've written the check and never missed it, Matt," said Doreen, giving me a frank stare.

"Then why did you say no?"

"First of all, because of the principle of the thing. Yeah, Kenny and Allie were our lifelong friends, but enough is enough. I was getting the sense that all I was doing was enabling the guy."

"And on top of that," I said, "forking over that kind of money could have blown your cover with David."

Doreen looked at me appreciatively. "Yes, Matt, that's right."

"So, what happened?"

"Nothing."

"Nothing?"

"I never heard another word about it."

"But you're starting to suspect that all this might be connected with David's disappearance."

"I don't know, Matt, but you know what they say: 'Follow the money.'"

"Thanks for telling me this, Doreen. This could be important."

"Do *you* think the two things might be connected, Matt?"

"I'm thinking it might be too much to be a coincidence for them not to be."

"Okay," she said, suddenly standing. "Enough of all this, let's go for a swim."

"Good idea."

We jumped in the pool and had a relaxing swim in the pool together. The cool water was refreshing and it helped ease the pain in my back. It also helped me clear my head, and, frankly, I needed the physical space from Doreen for a few minutes. But when we got out she sat down beside me on the chaise again.

"I gotta go," I said, as I toweled off my hair.

"Yeah, you do," said Doreen. Meaning what? "But before you go, could you do me a favor and put some sunblock on my back and shoulders? They're feeling burned."

"Sure," I said. I went over to a table where a container of the stuff was sitting and brought it back. She turned away from me so I could get to both her shoulders and I started to rub it in. Her skin was like satin, and the early summer sun had burnished it to gold. It was the same skin I'd admired at the pool all through high school. I wasn't sure it looked burned.

"Hang on a second," she said, and she reached up and nudged the straps of the bathing suit off her shoulders. "There," she said. She seemed to lean back into me just a little bit. I put some more lotion on my hands and began to rub it in. I thought I sensed her breathing begin to change. I knew mine had. I rubbed a little more. One of us moaned. Maybe it was me; maybe it wasn't. I never got a chance to find out.

Somewhere in the house a door slammed.

CHAPTER FOURTEEN

"MOM?" came a shout from inside the house.

"We're out by the pool!" Doreen shouted back as she jumped up from the chaise and hastily rearranged the straps on her bathing suit.

Donnie Chandler tumbled out the door the way all teenage boys do. He was a good-looking kid. He looked like his father. His straight blond hair was parted on the side, and it tended to fall over his forehead, just as David's always had. He wasn't as tall as David, maybe five-ten, but he was well built. He was wearing a pair of cutoffs and a Devon Central football jersey with the number 12 on it. David's number.

"Donnie," said Doreen, "this is Matt Hunter, an old friend of ours. Matt, this is our son, Donnie."

We shook hands awkwardly as I tried to put the polo shirt I'd worn over back on.

"Nice to meet you, Donnie," I said.

"Hey," he said, in a teenaged bass that would someday mellow to baritone.

"Where have you been off to?" said Doreen. After the morning we'd spent together, it was odd to hear her suddenly sound like a mother.

"I told you, Mom, me and the guys went to the pool."

"Was your sister there?"

"No, Mom, she has a tennis lesson this morning, remember?"

"Oh, that's right," said Doreen. "I can't keep up with the two of you anymore."

"So, Mr. Hunter," said Donnie, "you're the guy Dad threw all his passes to, huh?"

"Well, not all, but a lot of them," I said.

"It must have been a lot of fun playing on a team that good," said Donnie, perhaps a little wistfully.

"All I remember is how much fun it was playing football with my friends," I said, lying. Winning was good. Excelling was good. It was a feeling I'd all but forgotten.

"Look, guys," said Doreen, "it's almost 1 o'clock. Why don't I pull some stuff out of the fridge and we can have lunch together?"

"Sounds great, Mom," said Donnie. "I'm, like, starving."

"Sounds good," I said. I was, like, starving, too, but only the young can get away with saying it.

"Great," said Doreen. "Just give me a few minutes." She headed back toward the house and disappeared inside.

"So, Mr. Hunter," said Donnie. You wanna, like, toss the football around?"

"Sure," I said. I wasn't exactly dressed for it, and all I had for footwear was a pair of old running shoes, but they'd do.

"Cool," he said, and loped out through the pool gate to the back yard. I couldn't help noticing that, despite all the obvious similarities, Donnie seemed to lack a certain physical grace that David had always possessed, no matter what he'd been doing. I followed, not loping. There was a football sitting on a small bench just outside the gate, and Donnie picked it up.

David and Doreen had a large piece of property, and behind the pool there was a broad expanse of lawn that covered, I guessed, close to an acre. We tossed the ball around for a few minutes, mostly so that I could loosen up; Donnie appeared already loose and limber. He had a nice motion, but I couldn't help making a comparison between his throws and his father's. When David threw the ball, even when we were just tossing it around, it came at me with almost a hissing sound, and it stung my hands. I was one of the few guys who could handle his passes without risking broken fingers. Donnie had a nice spiral, and decent velocity, but that was about it. Maybe he was holding back.

"You wanna run a few routes?" I said.

"Cool," he said, smiling with a male version of Doreen's smile.

I started off with some short routes: button routes and crossing patterns. His throws were accurate and his velocity was decent, but even pushing forty I felt like he was leading me more than David ever did, and I didn't have to run as hard to catch up with them.

"Okay," I said. "Let's run a post pattern."

"Cool," he said, displaying the vast vocabulary of a teenage boy.

There were no yard markers, but I could pace off fifty yards in my sleep and come within a few inches of the exact distance. I took off down the field, cutting in at the same spot I always had, and looked up for the ball. It wasn't where it should have been. It seemed to be coming at me in slow motion, and even though I tried to adjust, it fell behind me and about ten yards short. I guess it was a decent throw for an average high school quarterback, but I'd never played with an average high school quarterback.

I jogged back and said, "Sorry. I guess I'm no good without yard markers. I ran that way too long."

"No problem," he said.

"Lunch is ready, guys!" shouted Doreen. She was standing at the pool yard fence and watching us with a smile on her face. She'd changed back into the slacks and blouse.

"Okay!" Donnie and I shouted back in unison.

"One more pass, okay?" said Donnie. "I hate to finish on an incomplete pass."

"So do I," I said. "How about a straight sprint pattern. Just throw it when you're ready."

"Cool," said Donnie.

I took off down the field running hard, but not as hard as I could. When David and I ran this route, David always waited until the last possible minute to throw the ball, until that exquisite instant when nobody else at the game except the two of us believed that he could get it to me. And then he'd launch a rocket, nailing me with it as I ran as hard as I could.

I'd barely run fifteen yards when I looked back. Donnie had already released the ball. It traced a long, lazy arc and I glided under it around 35 yards down the field and made the catch easily.

"Perfect!" I shouted.

"Yes!" I heard Donnie shout behind me.

"Good toss, Donnie," I said, as I jogged back to him.

"Man, that was the coolest," he said, beaming. "No wonder Dad loved playing with you so much. Thanks Mr. Hunter." We high-fived, a first for me, and headed back to the house.

Doreen had laid out cold cuts, deli salads, Kaiser rolls, and condiments, along with a pitcher of iced tea and a quart carton of milk.

"You guys have a good time?" said Doreen.

"The best, Mom," said Donnie. "Oh, man, this looks good," he said, as his male teenage brain instantaneously shifted all its attention to the food.

I had a sandwich, some coleslaw, and some iced tea. Doreen had the same, except she ate only half a sandwich. Donnie ate three sandwiches, about a pound of potato salad, and a forkful of coleslaw, probably just to please his mother. He washed it all down with the quart of milk. He'd just swallowed his last bite when the doorbell rang.

"Who could that be?" said Doreen.

"That's Pete and Rob," said Donnie, already heading for the door. "We're all headed back to the pool."

"Please give yourself a chance to digest your lunch before you go back in the water!" Doreen shouted. She gave me one of those, "what's a mother to do?" looks.

"Sure, Mom!" he shouted back as the door slammed.

"So, you and Donnie looked like you were having fun out there," said Doreen, as she began to clean up the kitchen.

"We were," I said, hoping she would drop the subject. She was silent for a few seconds, her hands resting on the counter, before I noticed that her shoulders seemed to be shaking. I looked closer. Her eyes were closed and there were tears running down her face.

I walked over to her, and before I could say a word she turned to me, put her arms around me, and buried her face in my chest.

"Oh, Matt," she said, "I'm so scared I can barely breathe."

"It's not time to be afraid yet," I said, not even convincing myself.

"I mean," she said, ignoring me, "I was looking out at you and Donnie, and it suddenly hit me: What if David's gone for good? What if that sweet little boy suddenly doesn't have his father?"

"Please, Doreen, let's not panic, okay?"

She looked up at me, but she didn't let go. "You have to find him, Matt. One way or another, you have to find him."

"I will, Doreen. I promise."

Her expression hardened. "You shouldn't promise, Matt. This isn't some football game."

"Okay. I won't promise. But I will find him."

She put her head back on my chest.

"Okay, Matt. Okay."

She suddenly broke away from me and started to walk from the room. Had I done something wrong? She returned a couple of minutes later holding a check.

"Look, Matt, I know you took on that other job because you needed the money. So please take this and don't argue with me," she said, handing me the check. I held it in my hand, but I didn't look at it. "We, my kids and I, can't afford to have you dividing your time. Please take this and promise me that you'll do nothing but look for David until you find him."

"That's a promise I can make, Doreen," I said, pocketing the check without arguing.

"Thank you," she said. She reached up on her toes and gave me a kiss on the lips. I think in the old days they would have called it a chaste kiss. But it was still kiss on the lips. "Now, get yourself out of here and get to work."

She put her arm around me and walked me to the door, and gave me another kiss before I left.

I barely remembered the drive back to the house. My mind was too crowded with images of Doreen to notice the road. I tried to think of how much trouble I was about to get into, how much humiliation I was setting myself up for, but nothing could erase the feeling of her skin under my fingers, or the sensation of her lips on mine. Chaste, my ass. Luckily, I knew the area like the back of my hand, and I didn't kill anybody on the way.

When I got home I pulled the check out of my pocket and looked at it. It was for $50,000.

I guessed Doreen didn't expect me to find her husband anytime soon.

CHAPTER FIFTEEN

"**Y**OU'RE KIDDING ME, RIGHT?" said my younger sister, standing in the kitchen and holding the coffee pot over my 1986 Mets cup. Nothing was sacred with her.

The morning had been going well until then, despite the fact that it was cloudy, and there was a foreboding touch of July humidity in the air.

I'd spent the night dreaming of Doreen, and I'd woken up feeling tired and disoriented. But a Sausage McMuffin and a large coffee from Mickey D's had cheered me up considerably, and I was cheered even further when I went to the bank and deposited Doreen's check.

Then Lacey ruined it all when she stopped by just after I'd gotten home and reminded me that I had to pay FICA and estimated income taxes on the money, and that I'd better pay off my credit card debt as well. I said I didn't know how to do all that, and she looked at me like a pumpkin was growing out of the top of my head.

"Sorry," I said.

"How did you do it the whole time you were practicing law?" she said.

"I kept all my receipts and bank records in a desk drawer, and at the end of the year I'd put the whole pile in a manila envelope and give it to Marianne's tax accountant."

"He must have loved that."

"He always said it really didn't make much difference one way or another, so he just took what I gave him and told me it was fine."

"Oh, Matt," was all she could say.

"So, what do I do?" I said.

"Give me a minute," she said.

She poured herself her cup of coffee and sat down at the table. She pulled her laptop out of the satchel that I never saw her without, opened it up, and started tapping the keys. She asked me for my Social Security number, my bank account number, and my credit card information, and otherwise ignored me. In less than half an hour she looked up.

"Okay," she said, "I've calculated your estimated federal and state income taxes and filed them electronically, and I also paid your FICA and cleared your credit card balance. When I get to a printer I'll print off hard copies for you which you must, I repeat, must, file away and not lose."

"Yes, ma'am," I said. "Thank you."

"And by the way, that $50,000 bank balance is now $28,795."

"What!?"

"Welcome to the real world, Sherlock."

"Thanks."

"Speaking of the real world," said Lacey, closing up her laptop and heading to the coffeepot for a refill, "how's your case going?"

I told her about my altercation with Eddie Shepherd and his girlfriend. She laughed at the story, but then she grew more serious.

"You know," she said, "I heard that Eddie's wife divorced him and left town with their two kids last year."

"I'm sorry to hear that," I said, surprised to find myself meaning it. "Was there someone else involved?"

"Yeah, it was some state cop from Newburgh."

"Ouch."

"Yeah, ouch," said Lacey. "I'm not saying that he's not an asshole, but everybody's got a story, you know?"

She grew even more somber when I told her that I'd gotten Eddie to send out the APB and the BOLO on David and his car; and she frowned as I recounted my visit to Doreen, and her revelations to me about the cash payments David had made to Allie over the years.

"I'm not surprised, Matt, but I am worried," she said when I'd finished.

"So am I. I think David could be in big trouble."

"I meant I'm worried about you."

"Me?"

"Yes, you."

"Why?"

"Look, Matt," said Lacey, putting her coffee cup down, finished with it for at least the moment, "you're going to have enough trouble getting yourself established in your job, and the last thing you should be doing is falling in love with your first client."

I thought I'd been talking about the case. I desperately tried to think back and recall anything I'd said that would have betrayed the feelings that I was developing for Doreen, but I came up empty. It wasn't the first time Lacey had seen right through me, but I didn't want to get into that discussion now, and not with my sister.

"What are you talking about?" I said, trying to sound shocked.

"Gimme a break, Matt," said Lacey, glaring.

"Lace, shouldn't we be talking about more important things than my love life, assuming there even is one?"

"Matt, if you start developing feelings for your client, it's going to affect how you pursue the case. You can't afford that, especially when you're trying to get yourself up and going, that's all."

"Look, Lacey, Doreen and I go way back. I think I can manage my feelings and help her out at the same time."

"I know all about how far back you and Doreen go, Matt, and I'm not so sure." She paused a moment and said, "You know, when I was in 6th grade, me and all the other girls wanted to be Doreen Carpenter. I mean, for chrissakes, she was the cheerleading captain, the Class President, the Prom Queen, the Homecoming Queen…"

"And she had the dreamiest boyfriend in the school, right?"

"Yes, Matt, yes she did. I might have been just a kid, but I could tell how much you liked her. I mean, she grew up two houses down from us. You grew up together. It must have been hard to accept the fact that she had feelings, the feelings you always wanted her to have for you, for someone else, especially when that someone else happened to be your best friend."

"Okay, let's say I don't disagree with you. But I don't see what that has to do with anything right now."

"When's the last time you got laid, Matt?"

"Jesus, Lacey," I said. I could feel myself turning red. "I don't think my sister is supposed to be asking me questions like that."

"Well, somebody has to. So, how long?"

"I don't know. A while, I guess."

"How long?"

"Look, it's been a couple of years, okay? Things haven't been good between Marianne and me for years, but I didn't want to be the one to break the promise."

"I'm proud of you for that, Matt."

"It's not much to be proud of, but I still don't know what you're getting at."

"Matt, if you haven't already, you're going to start imagining that she's returning the feelings you have for her."

"What if I'm not just imagining it?"

"Jesus, Matt," she said, shaking her head. "Trust me. You are."

"How do you know that?"

"Because, dear brother, you are a man. All men are children when it comes to their feelings about women, and children have lively imaginations."

"I think it's pretty unfair to say 'all men' are like that."

"Okay, I don't know all the men in the world, so you could theoretically be right."

I couldn't think of any way to respond to that, so I just laughed.

"Matt, I'm trying to be serious. You're starting a new life for yourself, both personally and professionally. Doreen Chandler is your client, a client who has paid you a lot of money to do a job for her. She is married to your best friend, and she loves him. Don't screw this up by trying to make it into anything more than that, okay?"

"Okay, Lacey," I said, "you're right."

"And besides, Matt, Doreen's really fragile right now, and you don't want to be exploiting that."

That one hit hard. Lacey was right, and I knew it. "You're right, Lace," I said. "I really mean it; you're right. I understand."

She gave me a skeptical look.

"Good," she said. "Now let's get back to business."

"Please, God, let's."

"So you think it's possible that this money that David's been funneling to Allie is about Kenny's gambling?"

"I don't know, but let's just say I don't find it unbelievable."

"At least it's a lead. You need to chase that down. If Kenny's gotten himself into trouble with some bad guys, they may have found out where the money was really coming from and gone right to the source. David may be hiding from them."

"It sounds like Doreen should be the one hiding from them, if Kenny's gambling really is the problem here."

"Yeah," said Lacey, "except Doreen's kept a pretty good lid on the money stuff. I think just about everybody really believes the 'David Chandler, Prosperous Banker' story."

"You're probably right. Do you think I should confront Kenny?"

"No, I don't."

"Why not? I'm one of his best friends. Maybe I can get him to talk to me about it."

"Gamblers are like drunks and dope addicts, Matt. They lie. They lie to themselves, and they lie to everyone else, especially their best friends and their loved ones. I don't care how good a friend Kenny is. If he's got a gambling problem he's going to lie about it, to you and to everyone else, and talking to him isn't going to get you anywhere."

I knew my sister had learned that lesson the hard way, and I wasn't about to argue with her.

"So what do I do?"

Lacey stood up and left the room without any explanation. I knew better than to follow. In a few minutes she came back.

"Are you hungry?"

"What does that have to do with anything?"

"I said, are you hungry?"

I looked at my watch. I felt like I'd just left McDonald's but it was already noon. My stomach started to grumble at the sudden realization.

"Yes, I'm hungry."

"Good. Come with me." She picked up her laptop, put it away, and headed for the door.

Having nothing better to do, I followed her.

"We're taking your car," she said, looking over her shoulder.

"Fine," I said, meaning it. I always prefer to drive when I'm in a car, and I have a thing against being seen in 1993 Saturns.

CHAPTER SIXTEEN

ANTHONY FORNAIO STILL SMELLED FAINTLY OF RISING DOUGH.

Lacey and I had driven into town and parked close to Franco's, now formally known as "Il Cuccina della Torino." But instead of going in the front door, Lacey led me around to the back and knocked on a door to a service entrance near a couple of dumpsters. After a few seconds the door groaned open.

Anthony had a shy smile and a heavy beard; it was only noon and he already had a five o'clock shadow. He'd probably gained sixty pounds since high school, but he seemed to carry it well, and his dark hair was still thick and curly, giving him a certain boyishness. His eyes were lively, clear, and intelligent, exuding kindness and wit.

"I hope you don't mind an uninvited guest," said Lacey, giving him a hug and a little kiss on the cheek.

"A friend of yours is a friend of mine, Lacey," he said, "even this guy. It's good to see you Matt. It's been a long time." He extended a floury hand and I shook it.

"It's good to see you, too, Anthony," I said. "It's quite a place you've got here."

"What, you mean out front there?" he said, waving his arm vaguely.

"Well, yeah," I said. "It certainly isn't the Franco's I remember."

"It isn't the Franco's I remember, either," he said.

"It seems to be doing great, though."

"Oh, yeah, it's doing great," said Anthony, a little dismissively. "I can't argue with the decision Pop made. We put a lot of money into the old place and hired a first-rate executive chef out of New York. It's really worked out well for us. The town's changed since we were growing up, Matt. A place like this wouldn't have lasted a month back then. But now? We're booked two weeks in advance all the time."

"But you still miss the old place," I said.

"Well, yes and no," he said. "Come with me."

He led Lacey and me down a dim hallway and into a small room off the main kitchen. It had just enough space for a pizza oven, a counter, and a few tables. It had no windows, but seemed to be well ventilated and was comfortably lit.

"This is my place," he said. "I let Alphonse, the chef, run the front of the house. I manage the payroll and the suppliers and generally keep an eye on things, but that's about it. This is my baby."

"It smells like old times, Anthony," I said, inhaling the aroma.

"Yeah, it does, doesn't it?"

"Is that the original oven from the old place?" I said.

"Good eye, Matt," giving me a surprised smile. "Yes, it is, and it still works like it was new."

"Do you do a lot of business back here?"

"Eh," he said with a shrug, "it's not here for business, y'know? I don't do take out and it's not open to the public. It's just my private place where I invite friends, like your sister." He looked over at Lacey with soft eyes and a warm smile. I saw Lacey blush for the first time in my life.

"Then thanks for having me here," I said.

He nodded and said, "So, can I make you a pie?"

"Oh, man, you sure can," I said. "How about pepperoni, mushrooms and sausage?"

"The Holy Trinity," he said.

"Could you put anchovies on half?" said Lacey.

"See?" said Anthony. "Your sister knows that anchovies are what make pizza a health food."

"All I know is they taste good," said Lacey, as she filled a glass with Coke from a drink dispenser.

"Put 'em on the whole thing," I said. "I love anchovies."

"That's right, you do," said Anthony. "You were the only kid I knew back then besides me who always ordered anchovies on his pizza."

"I guess I got out of the habit when I got married."

"These things happen," said Anthony, mournfully. Clearly a world that valued marriages over anchovies was a world gone mad.

"Yet another good reason for the divorce," said Lacey.

"Why don't you pour yourself a drink and sit down while I get to work," said Anthony, tactfully not rising to Lacey's bait.

We chitchatted back and forth while he went about his cooking, and in no time he put the steaming pie on the table, grabbed himself a drink, and sat down with us.

I bit into my first slice and was transported back to my youth. I'd lived and worked in New York City for years, and I'd eaten a lot of great pizza, but I'd never had anything that tasted like Franco's pizzas, most of which Anthony had made, even back then. The crust was superb: thin, but not hard like thin crusts can get. The mozzarella was fresh, moist and tasty, and the meats and tomato sauce were bursting with flavor. The anchovies were salty and tangy, tasting fresh from the sea but not fishy. I ate a quarter of the pie, and so did Anthony. My skinny sister ate the rest and finished about the same time Anthony and I did.

"I try as hard as I can to fatten her up," said Anthony, "but I'm not making any progress."

"Keep trying," said Lacey, wiping her mouth with a napkin.

Anthony picked up the empty pie plate and reached over to the counter to deposit it. "Now," he said, his expression gone suddenly serious, "we talk."

"Matt," said Lacey, "You have to understand that whatever is said here stays here. Anthony has agreed to talk to you because of our friendship, and because I promised him that he could trust you. It would be a personal betrayal if you ever repeated a word of what we are about to discuss. Do you understand?"

I looked at Anthony and for the first time noticed a hard intelligence in those soft eyes. Maybe we'd all been wrong about Anthony Fornaio.

I met his gaze and said, "I understand."

He nodded and said, "I understand that you suspect your old friend Kenny Cooper may have a gambling problem, and that this may be related to the peculiar disappearance of your friend David Chandler."

"Yes," I said. "I've been looking for David for over a week, and so far it's the only lead I've been able to come up with."

"You must understand, Matt, that I'm not personally involved in the gambling business or in any other illegal activities. This place," he said, waving his arm around the small room, his eyes resting on Lacey, "and the friends who come here, are my world. That's all. Do you understand, Matt?"

"I understand."

"Good," he said. "But, Matt, I also have relatives. You were an NYPD cop, so perhaps you already know that."

Oh. Those Fornaios. I should have made the connection long ago, but I hadn't. I nodded like I'd known all along.

"Your sister has explained to me the amounts of money that have made you suspicious, and I think that if Kenny, or anyone else around here, was betting that kind of money, my relatives would probably know about it, especially my Uncle Tommy."

AKA Tommassino Fornaio, who, last time I looked, oversaw all mob-related activity in New York State north of The Bronx. I felt my testicles starting to retract like they were trying to find someplace to hide.

"Oh," I said.

"Perhaps you'd like to speak to him personally about the matter," said Anthony. "As I said, I really don't want to be involved."

"I understand, Anthony, but your uncle must be a busy man."

"Yes, he is," said Anthony, "but he'll make time for you."

"Are you sure Anthony? That would be great," I said, thinking of how many ways this could turn out to be not so great.

"I'm sure," said Anthony. He looked at the clock on the wall and said, "As a matter of fact, he is expecting you and your sister in an hour."

"I don't know what to say," I said, because I really didn't. "Thank you."

"Your sister will take you there," said Anthony. "Please don't go without her. And Matt?"

"Yes, Anthony."

"My uncle is a very kind man, but he is also not to be trifled with."

"I understand," I said.

"Good," he said, looking at me with his kind eyes and giving me a warm smile. "Good."

CHAPTER SEVENTEEN

"**D**ON'T ASK, DO YOU HEAR ME? Just don't ask," said my sister as we drove up Route 9W toward Newburgh. "You know the rule."

"I know, Lace," I said. "No questions about your past. I understand. But, geez."

"Geez, nothing. Now, make a left at the next light."

We took another left and then a right. Before long we were in a nice, upper-middle class neighborhood on the outskirts of Newburgh. It was an older neighborhood, with houses built mostly of brick or stone. Too many of these neighborhoods had been allowed to deteriorate over the years, but this one had held up well. The houses and the small yards were all beautifully maintained, and late-model, upscale cars were parked in the short driveways.

We parked on the street, and Lacey walked ahead of me up to the front door of one of the nicest houses on the block. She rang the doorbell and I heard the sound of deep chimes emanate from inside the house. In just a few seconds the door opened and, to my utter astonishment, Tommassino Fornaio himself welcomed us into his home.

Perhaps it's because I own the entire "Sopranos" collection on DVD, or that I'd read "The Godfather" from cover to cover a dozen times. Or perhaps not. Whatever the reason, Tommassino Fornaio was not what I expected.

He was a shorter than I was, a little under six feet, slender, with a full head of well-tended blond hair just going gray around the temples. I guessed he was an extremely well preserved sixty. He was wearing a yellow Izod golf shirt, khaki-colored Dockers, and a pair of tasseled loafers over yellow argyle socks. He was clean-shaven and smelled of expensive aftershave. He was the picture of a successful insurance executive headed out for an afternoon of golf with important clients. But he was thug, a big one, and I couldn't allow myself to forget that.

"Uncle Tommy!" said Lacey, throwing her arms around him.

"Lacey dearest," said Fornaio, in a soft voice, hugging her in return. Then he held her at arms length and said, "You're looking marvelous, sweetheart. It's wonderful to see you."

"It's been too long," said Lacey, beaming, while I stood there feeling like an uninvited vacuum cleaner salesman who'd snuck in behind her.

Perhaps sensing my discomfort, Fornaio turned to me and said, "Hello, Matt. What a pleasure to meet you after all these years. I was a big fan."

"It's a pleasure to meet you, too, Sir," I said.

"Ah, 'Sir,' nothing. Call me Tommy," he said, leading us into a large, bright room decorated with comfortable but expensive looking furniture. "Come on in and make yourself at home. Can I get you some coffee?"

"Sure," Lacey and I said in unison, although my nerves were jangling.

He picked up a phone and, without dialing, said, "We'd like some coffee in the living room. Thanks," and hung up.

We were just getting settled when a stunning woman walked into the room. She was dressed casually in slacks, a blouse, and a scarf. A pair of sunglasses sat perched atop elegantly coiffed honey-colored hair.

"Lacey!" she said as she walked over to her and exchanged air kisses. "So lovely to see you. And you must be Lacey's brother Matt," she said, turning to me as I stood. She reached out and clasped my hand in a warm, firm grip. "I'm Christina, Tommy's wife."

"A pleasure to meet you, ma'am," I said. The simple arithmetic told me that she, too, had to be at least sixty, but she didn't look a day over forty-five, if that. I tried not to stare.

Tony and Carmela they were not.

Tommassino Fornaio, as I recalled reading somewhere, long ago, had arrived from Sicily as a stowaway at the age of six. He'd grown up hard on the Lower East Side, in a part of what was then Little Italy, but what was now part of the ever-expanding Chinatown. He'd been raised by a great-aunt and uncle whom his family in Sicily had told him lived in New York, but whom he had never met.

But Tommy, as he'd insisted on being called from the day he set foot on American soil, was as smart as he was tough. He taught himself to speak fluent English in six months, and refused to speak his native Sicilian to anyone except his great-aunt and uncle, out of respect, although he reputedly still spoke it perfectly.

He went to public schools, graduating near the top of his high school class, and then on to the City College of New York, where he'd majored in economics and again graduated near the top of his class.

He married his childhood sweetheart, Christina; they both became naturalized citizens and set out to live the American Dream.

But then Tommassino Fornaio hit the rock-hard wall of reality.

Even in the enlightened 1970's, the banking and financial industries of New York were still bastions of the WASP elite, and Italian immigrants, whom the elite still called "wops" and "goombahs" in the quiet lounges of their private clubs, were not welcome. Door after door was slammed in young Tommy's face before he could even get a foot inside. Letters and phone calls went unanswered.

So, Tommy Fornaio took what he had and ran with it. Using connections his family had back in the old country, and other connections that he'd made growing up in Little Italy, Tommy went into business the old-fashioned way, on the wrong side of the legal railroad tracks.

But he had one rule that he would never break: He would not ply his trade within the Five Boroughs of New York City. He lived by this rule for two reasons: The first was simply survival. The five boroughs were already controlled by long-established families, and he knew he wouldn't last long on their turf. They liked the young man, but business was business, and Tommy knew they would kill him without hesitation if he became a problem. But they would leave him alone, and even subsidize him, north of the city limits, an area about which they knew little and in which they had no interest. For Tommy, that first reason was simply common sense, a practical matter.

But the second reason was personal.

Tommassino Fornaio would never forget the personal rejection, the snubs, and the slights that both he, and more importantly, his beautiful young wife had endured when they had tried to begin their life together respectably in Manhattan, and he would extract his revenge. But not revenge the old Sicilian way: the American way. He would return to Manhattan one day as a successful, legitimate businessman. His children would go to school with the children of the bankers who had closed their doors to him. He and his wife would share drinks with those same bankers and their wives at their cherished clubs; and they would attend the same gala fundraisers as those people, where their money would be as good as anybody else's, and their generosity would be met with gratitude, not insults. Those people would smile their ingratiating smiles and gladly shake his hand, and gratefully kiss his wife on her lovely cheek.

But to do all that, Tommy had to stay clean in New York City. It wouldn't be difficult. New York City was essentially a village, and its wealthy residents' provincials to the bone beneath their veneers of urbanity, provincials who didn't know and didn't care what went on outside the city boundaries, where Tommy would be free to pursue his fortune in his own way. But in New York, especially Manhattan, he had to stay clean, immaculate. He owned three luxury car dealerships in Manhattan and maintained a townhouse on 5th Avenue overlooking Central Park.

Apparently, it had worked.

Christina Fornaio turned to Tommassino and said, "Okay, Tommy, I'm off. I hope you haven't forgotten that I have that charity auction to attend tonight at the Waldorf, so I won't be home until around eleven."

"I haven't forgotten, dear. Anyway, I'm having dinner with the Mayor tonight, so we'll probably be getting home about the same time."

"Good," she said. "Perhaps we can have a cup of coffee and watch the news together when we get home."

"Sounds lovely," he said.

"So nice to see you, Lacey," she said. "Please don't be a stranger." She turned her stunning green eyes on me and said, "It was a pleasure to meet you, Matt."

"The pleasure was all mine," I said.

She breezed out of the room just as a maid entered bearing a silver tray holding a coffee pot, cups, and cream and sugar. She deposited it on a mahogany table and quietly left in Christina's wake.

"Who is the mayor of Newburgh, now?" I said.

Tommassino gave me a puzzled look, and after a brief pause, said, "The Mayor of Newburgh is Frank Harris. Why do you ask?"

"I'm sorry. I haven't had a chance to catch up with local politics. It's just that you said you were going out to dinner with him tonight."

"With Frank?" he said. "Oh! I'm sorry. No, I'm not going to dinner with Frank; I'm going to dinner with the Mayor of New York City. We get together every couple of months to catch up, just the two of us. I own a little restaurant in the Bronx that's about halfway between us. The Mayor loves the veal piccata there, and it's always a pleasant evening."

"I'm sure," I said.

"Now, Matt," he said as he poured coffee for all of us, "I'm told that you are concerned that one of your oldest friends may be getting himself into some trouble with gambling. An old teammate of yours named Kenneth Cooper."

"That's right."

"And you are concerned not just for him personally, but also because you believe his gambling may somehow be related to the disappearance of another one of your old friends, David Chandler."

"Yes, Sir."

"Please, it's Tommy."

"Yes, Tommy."

"I remember the three of you fondly from your football days," he said, sitting back and smiling. He took a sip of his coffee. "You guys used to put on quite a show."

"I guess we did," I said. "I just remember the fun of it."

"Excellence is its own reward, isn't it?" he said, looking directly at me. "And mediocrity is its own punishment."

"I guess that's about as well as I've ever heard it put," I said, the words striking home hard.

"We must never accept mediocrity from ourselves," he said, his remarkable blue eyes still on me, "especially when we have already proven ourselves to be capable of more."

"No, we shouldn't," I said.

"Now," he said, putting his coffee cup down. He sat forward and clasped his hands. "I generally don't make it my business to meddle in other people's affairs. People are free to do what they want with their hard-earned money. Some people want a nice car; some people perhaps want a vacation home, or a boat. Others like to eat at fancy restaurants and drink expensive wine. Everybody's different, and that's what makes the world an interesting place, right?"

I nodded.

"And," he said, unclasping his hands and extending his arms out to his sides, "some people like to gamble, and they like to do it without the government nosing into their affairs. Who can blame them? It's a private matter, and, frankly, it's against the rules that I live by to discuss other people's private matters. But in this case, I know you feel that there might possibly be a life at stake, and that's a serious concern. So, in light of the seriousness of the issue, and in light of my high regard for your sister, I've decided to make an exception in this case."

"I really appreciate that, Uncle Tommy," said Lacey.

"It's all right, my dear," he said, waving off the comment. "I know you never would have asked me if it wasn't important. Normally I wouldn't get personally involved in transactions this small, but I made some calls. I inquired about any potential activity your friend may have engaged in in the local area, and I also made inquiries about any potential activities in the Greater New York and Tri-State areas. The people I spoke to were reliable people. And I can tell you that your friend Kenny Cooper is not a gambler. He doesn't even buy lottery tickets."

"Then why would Kenny's wife have said that he was?" I said, stunned. It was the one answer I hadn't been looking for.

"That's a private matter between a husband and his wife," said Fornaio. "You'll have to talk to one of them."

"Well," I said, "I guess that raises more questions than it answers, but it's very helpful, and I thank you." I rose to leave, and so did Lacey. This was not a man whose time I felt I should waste.

"Please, sit back down," said Fornaio. "Sadly, we have another matter to discuss."

I sat back down. I thought back once again to all those "Godfather" movies. Was this going to be one of those, "Your Godfather is going to ask a favor of you in return" moments? Would this be the moment when I would be put on notice that I was to be at this man's beck and call for the rest of my life? What had I gotten myself into?

"About a month ago," he said, "I received a phone call from an acquaintance. He told me that a man had come to him requesting a private loan in the amount of $150,000. As I've said, I normally would never get involved personally in a transaction so trivial; but the man asking for the loan was a prominent member of his community, a local hero, a man with whom I had occasionally played golf at charity tournaments. It was a delicate situation, so this acquaintance did me the courtesy of requesting my advice and counsel."

"Oh, no," I said.

"I'm sorry to say that you are right, Matt. It was your friend, David Chandler."

"If you don't mind my asking, did he get the money?"

"No, he did not."

"But why?"

"That is not your concern, Matt."

"Did he tell you why he needed it?"

"Matt," said Lacey. "Stop."

"It's okay," said Fornaio, raising his hand. "It's okay, this once." He looked directly at me. "I've already broken some of my strictest rules of conduct, and I've gone as far as I'm willing to go, even for a friend. Now it's up to you, Matt. It's like football: You either take to the field and lead, or you are merely a spectator. You are either up to this task or you are not. If you are, you will find out what you need to know to help your friend. If you are not, then you will have to step aside and let someone else more capable do it. I hope it will be the former."

"I understand," I said. "Thank you for all you've done, and I hope you accept my apologies for my rudeness."

"Think nothing of it," said Tommassino, smiling. He rose. He shook my hand and gave Lacey an affectionate hug, and then he ushered us to the door.

Lacey and I drove back to my house in silence.

But as I drove, I couldn't help asking myself why Tommassino Fornaio, a thug, had been able to awaken in me that long dormant will to win, that irresistible urge to be the best that I could be no matter what the endeavor, that had slumbered within me for so long.

I had a lot to think about.

CHAPTER EIGHTEEN

I WAS SAVORING AN EGG MCMUFFIN and a large cup of coffee at McDonald's the next morning when Lacey walked in. She grabbed herself a cup of coffee at the counter and took a seat opposite me.

"The classics never go out of style, do they?" she said, staring at my Egg McMuffin.

"I like to vary my diet, you know?" I said.

"Yeah, I know all about your varied diet."

"That's kind of the pot calling the kettle black, isn't it, Lace?"

"It probably is. But, hey, as long as we both focus on health foods I guess it's okay, right?"

"That's how I see it," I said, dead serious. Between pizza and Egg McMuffins, I figured I was getting a pretty balanced diet as long as I got green peppers on the pizza now and then. "So anyway, how did you find me here?"

"It's not exactly hard, Matt. You weren't home. Where else would you be?"

"You have a point. So what's up?"

"Hang on a second," she said, standing up. "That bad boy looks good. I've gotta have one."

She came back in a few minutes with her sandwich and two fresh coffees.

"I'm assuming you didn't come here for the sole purpose of critiquing my diet," I said.

"No, I didn't," she said. "I came here because I feel stupid."

"That must be a first for you," I said.

"In my dreams," she said. "I feel stupid because I missed something obvious, and it might be slowing down your case."

"What's that?" I said, putting down my sandwich. Lacey had already finished hers.

"Remember when I set up your website for you, how I told you that the search engine that you use will locate where you are so that it can narrow your searches to a specific region?"

"Yeah, I remember, "I said. "Like when I searched for "private investigators" it narrowed the search to the local area automatically."

"That's right. And the search engines and the sites you log onto will do that unless you expressly disallow them. That way they can target news and local ads that are relevant to you."

"Okay. So what's the point?"

"The point is that I think I recall you telling me that when you visited David's office his laptop wasn't there, and that Angie Forrester told you that he always took it home with him."

"That's right."

"So what if he took it with him wherever he went? And what if he's been logging onto it?"

"I never thought of that."

"Don't take this the wrong way, Matt, but I never would have expected you to. But I damn well should have expected myself to."

"So, can you find out if he's been using his laptop?"

"Yes, I could, but I'd prefer to do this on the up and up if we can. That's a pretty serious form of hacking and, frankly, it would be faster and easier to do this by the rules."

"So how do I do that?"

"You go to the Orange County Bank and Trust and ask for their cooperation. You won't have a search warrant, of course, but perhaps they'll be willing to help you out."

I looked at my watch. "Angie Forrester will be there by now. You want to come with me? I don't know if I'd be able to ask the right questions about all this stuff."

"Uh, sure," said Lacey, after only a brief hesitation.

"Good," I said, taking a final sip of my coffee. "Let's go."

******

Angie Forrester came out to greet us looking spectacular in a close-fitting red dress, a simple string of pearls, and a pair of black heels that made her taller than I was. It was probably unprofessional of me, but I couldn't help noticing that she wasn't wearing a wedding ring, a detail I hadn't noticed before. It could have been because my detecting skills had improved since the last time I saw her. It also could have been because the dress ended above her knees and her legs looked terrific.

Joanne hadn't seemed as pleased to see me as she had been the last time, probably because I'd shown up without an appointment. Or perhaps it was the faded jeans and Todd Rundgren tee shirt that Lacey was wearing. In any event, she had reluctantly agreed to ask Angie if she could spare a moment for us, and a few moments later she had returned, grudgingly, with Angie.

Angie greeted us both warmly, apparently not offended by Lacey's tee shirt –perhaps she was a Rundgren fan – and invited us into her office. She offered us coffee, which Lacey immediately accepted, but I declined. I'd already had two cups and I didn't want to have to make an embarrassing mid-conversation dash to the men's room.

"I was hoping," she said, while she poured the coffee, "that you'd come with good news about David, but judging by your expressions I gather that's not the case."

"I'm sorry to say that you are correct," I said.

"I'm sorry, too," she said. "It's been over a week now, and that can't be good. Do you have any leads at all?"

"The only lead we have is that it might involve money somehow."

"That doesn't sound like David," said Angie.

"No, it doesn't," I said. "I hate to ask you this, but can I assume that he hadn't applied for a loan here in the past couple of months?" I said.

"Yes, you can. I know that because it is strictly against bank policy to loan money to employees."

"He might have been desperate and asked anyway," I said.

"If he had, it would have been reported to me. He absolutely did not apply for a loan here. But I could have answered that question over the phone, so I'm assuming you didn't drive all the way over here just to ask it."

"You're right," I said. "I asked Lacey to come with me because we have a request to make regarding David's computer equipment, and Lacey has some expertise in that area that I don't."

"Neither do I," said Angie. "Hang on a second." She made a quick phone call, and in a few minutes a disheveled looking young man wearing worn khakis and a shirt and tie that didn't match entered her office.

"This is Brad Schmidt, our Chief Information Officer," she said. "Brad, I'd like you to meet Matt Hunter and his sister, Lacey."

"Nice to meet you, Brad," I said.

"Nice to meet you, too," he said. He then turned to Lacey with a wary expression and said, "Lacey."

"Brad," said Lacey, her face set in stone.

Angie and I exchanged a glance.

"Brad," said Angie before things could get worse, "David Chandler apparently dropped out of sight about a week ago. Matt has been hired by his wife to find him, and he came here looking for our assistance. He brought his sister with him because she has expertise in the area of computers and computer networks."

"Apparently," said Brad. He and Lacey eyed each other like two boxers circling each other in the first round of a championship match.

"Brad," said Lacey, "We're here to ask a favor."

"How lovely," he said.

"Brad, look," said Lacey. "We were wondering if you would be able to tell us if David Chandler has logged on to his computer in the past week, and, if he has, would you be able to backtrack his activity and tell us where he was when he was logged on."

"We normally don't provide that information," said Brad.

"We're not looking for any of his personal information or any network information related to his computer or the bank's network. We just want to know if he's logged on to the computer and where he was when he did."

"How charming of you to ask," said Brad.

"Brad," said Angie, "it's completely up to you, but I would appreciate it if you could help them."

He stared at Lacey a few seconds longer and then turned to Angie. "Okay. May I please use your computer?"

"Go ahead."

Brad sat down at Angie's computer and started to tap on the keys. His typing didn't have the same confident speed and rhythm that Lacey's had, but he didn't hesitate, and he seemed to know what he was doing. In a few minutes he looked up.

"Sorry," he said, "David Chandler hasn't logged on to his computer since last Wednesday, and all that activity took place while he was here in this building."

"Could you tell us," I said, "if any of the activity looks like it could have been non-bank related business? Does any of it look suspicious to you?"

Brad looked at Angie, who nodded silently. He then spent a few more minutes clicking and tapping, then looked up.

"No. It's all just mundane bank stuff. I went back a couple of days, too. Still nothing. The guy wrote almost no emails, and he received even fewer."

"Is it possible that he had a private email address that nobody but he knew about?"

"Of course it's possible. But if he logged on to it using his company computer, I would have been able to see the activity. As I'm sure your sister would know," he added, giving Lacey a dirty look.

I was starting to think that the sooner I wrapped this up the better.

"Thank you so much, both of you," I said. "I have just one last request. Could you check periodically and tell us if there is any activity?"

Brad looked at Angie one more time. She gave him another silent nod.

"Sure," he said. He gave Lacey another hard stare. "It's not like it would matter all that much, would it?"

"Cut it out, Brad," said Lacey.

"All right then," said Angie. "Brad, thank you so much." He nodded to her and to me but not to Lacey. He left the room quickly.

I thanked Angie profusely and got us out of the bank as quickly as possible.

"What the hell was that all about?" I said, when we were back in the car.

"What was what all about?"

"Come on, Lace. Don't play games."

She turned away from me and looked straight ahead.

"You know the rules," she said.

CHAPTER NINETEEN

"I GUESS I SHOULDN'T BE SURPRISED," said Allison Cooper as she stared at me through the screen door. It was raining out, the first rain since I'd gotten back to Devon-on-Hudson, and my stomach was killing me.

Despite my devotion to a simple, health-oriented diet, I also believed firmly that variety is the spice of life. So I'd skipped McDonald's that morning and gone to a local diner instead to satisfy my periodic craving for poached eggs and corned beef hash. I'd ordered rye toast and a side of home fries to balance out the nutritional content, and now I was paying for it. It must have been the onions in the potatoes. My stomach didn't seem to tolerate onions the way it used to. But what are home fries without onions?

"Hi, Allison," I said, suppressing a belch. "Long time."

"Long time," she said, making no move to invite me in.

"I was hoping you might have a few minutes to talk."

"I'm sure you were," she said, still making no move to open the door.

"I won't take much of your time."

"No, you won't."

"Allie, please."

"Okay," she said, after making me wait a few more long seconds. "I guess I can't leave you standing out there in the rain. And besides, you look like you could use some Tums."

"How could you tell?" I said as I stepped into a tall-ceilinged foyer.

"Are you kidding me? The way Kenny eats and drinks, I buy the stuff by the case. His snoring is bad enough, never mind having him getting up every half hour because of his heartburn. I'll be right back."

She looked pretty good walking away. Allie had always been one of those slender people that you just knew would never gain any weight. She was small, and she'd never had any bust to speak of. But her hair was still the jet black of her youth; her face was unlined and still pretty in its own way, and whatever she'd had twenty years ago that had made her attractive was still there. A disturbing image of her and enormous Kenny in bed together settled into my imagination and wouldn't go away. She returned with a glass of water and three Tums.

"I'd offer you coffee," she said, handing me the glass and the tablets, "but I don't think I'd be doing you any favors if I did."

"That's fine," I said, looking around the house as I chewed on the Tums. "I really don't mean to stay long, anyway."

"Come on in and sit down," she said, leading me into a spacious living room.

It was a larger home than I'd expected. Not in the same category as David and Doreen's house by any means, but it must have cost a pretty penny.

"What? Did you think we'd be living in a double-wide?" said Allie, catching me as I glanced around.

"No, no. I was just taking in the place. It's nice."

"Thanks, but you're thinking we can't afford it, not on Kenny's pay."

"I have no idea what Kenny's being paid as A.D., but I assume he's doing pretty well. It's a big job."

"Give me a break," said Allison. "Big job? There never was such a thing as an Athletic Director before they made up the job for Kenny."

"I know there wasn't one when I was here," I said, trying to ignore the implication, "but I thought that maybe with the size of the school district now, they decided they needed one."

"What they decided was they had to get Kenny out of the head coaching job before he completely destroyed the football program. Nobody had the heart to fire him, so they created the job."

"Does Kenny know that?"

"You'd have to ask Kenny what he knows or doesn't know, but I doubt it. Kenny's in his own world, you know?"

"Do they at least pay him well?"

"They pay him squat." She pulled out a pack of Newport cigarettes and lit one up, something I'd never seen her do. She took a long drag and looked me in the eye. "Which brings us to why you're here, doesn't it?"

"Look, Allie, I'm sure you know by now that David's been gone for more than a week, and you probably know that Doreen's hired me to find him."

"Yeah, Kenny told me."

"And in the course of our conversations, it came up that you'd gone to David over the years for some, you know, financial assistance."

Allie was quiet for a long time. She took one last long drag on her cigarette and stubbed it out hard in an ashtray. "Your conversations with Doreen?"

"Yes."

"Oh."

"I'm sorry, Allie. I'm confused."

"I thought the loans were a private matter between me and David, that's all. He knew I didn't want Doreen to know. I thought maybe you found out about them by looking at his bank records or something. He's the big shot banker with all the money. I guess I thought he'd worked it all out without Doreen knowing."

So Doreen's secret had been well kept.

"I'm sorry, Allie."

"It's just, you know, it's kind of humiliating, that's all." She wiped away a tear from the corner of her eye.

"Allie, did Kenny know about the money?"

"Of course not," she said, her eyes suddenly dry, the hard façade returning. "Kenny's completely stupid about money. He actually believes that we can live the way we do on his salary." She laughed, but there was no humor in it.

"So you needed the money to maintain your lifestyle?"

"Something like that."

"Doreen told me that a few months ago you asked David for more money than you'd ever asked for in the past. She said you asked for $150,000. David seemed to imply to her that Kenny had gotten himself into gambling problems. She also told me that David turned you down."

She looked at me in shock. "She said that?"

"Yes, she did."

"What a bunch of crap."

"What?"

"I said that was a bunch of crap. What part of that didn't you understand?"

"I meant," I said, trying to remain patient, "were you referring to the part about the gambling or the part about how David turned you down?"

"Kenny doesn't gamble; he never has. He spends all his free time drinking beer with his buddies. Gambling doesn't interest him, I think mostly because it confuses him."

"So, what did you need that much money for?"

"Personal expenses," she said.

"What do you mean, 'personal expenses'?"

"I mean personal expenses," she said, giving me a look that said, "Move on."

"Did you ever go to anyone else for money?"

"Of course not."

"Why, 'of course not'?"

"Because remember what that bank robber used to say when they asked him why he robbed banks?"

"It was Willie Sutton. He said, 'because that's where the money is.'"

"Correct. David makes a ton, and, besides, Kenny's his best friend, especially since you got out of Dodge. Why shouldn't he share?"

"Allie, $150,000 is a lot of money, even for David," I said, perpetuating the fiction.

"Perhaps."

"So were you disappointed when he turned you down?"

Allie took another cigarette from the pack, lit it, and took a long drag, expelling the smoke slowly. She gave me a long, level look.

"Who said he turned me down?" she said.

CHAPTER TWENTY

L ACEY LIVED IN A LOFT over a small factory out near where Interstate 84 and the New York State Thruway intersect. The company operating the factory was called MainLine, Inc., and it manufactured fuel injection systems for high-performance cars. It looked busy and prosperous, but the name made me wonder how my sister had gotten to know the owners. I decided I didn't really want to know. The loft was really nothing more than an open area with a massive computer workstation, a bed that would make a cot look comfortable, and a couple of chairs that looked like they'd been stolen from Goodwill. But it was well lit by a large skylight and Lacey kept it immaculate. The air conditioning from the factory floor kept it cool, although some of the machinery noise leaked in. Lacey didn't seem to mind.

"So, Lacey," I said, looking around, "where do you cook and, you know, shower?"

"I eat out, Matt," she said. "At the time in my life when I should've been learning from Mom how to cook I was kind of otherwise engaged. As for the showers, the owner has a full bathroom suite attached to his office, and he lets me use it."

"Pretty Spartan," I said.

"It suits me fine," said Lacey.

"You say so," I said. I didn't have any idea what Lacey made, but I'd hoped it would be enough for her to live a little better than this. "So, anyway, how do you think David got that kind of money?" I said, after I'd told her about my visit with Allison Cooper.

"She could be lying, you know," she said.

"About what?"

"About everything. She was clearly lying to you when she said the only reason she needed the money was for 'personal expenses.' There has to be more to it than that."

"I don't know, Lace. They live in an awfully nice house in an expensive neighborhood."

"That's my point," she said. "It just doesn't make sense. Why would David Chandler hand over that kind of money, year after year, just to keep his friend in that kind of lifestyle, especially when he had to go begging to his wife to get it? It seems to me that there are limits, even to a close friendship. If David were really a friend, he should have talked to Kenny and told him that he should sell the fancy house and live a life more in line to his income."

"Kenny didn't know about the money, Lace."

"That's what makes the whole thing smell even more. Why did this all happen between Allie and David?"

"I think they were both trying to protect Kenny, that's all."

"I don't know, Matt. It just doesn't sound right to me. And why did Doreen put up with it for so long?"

"I guess that's a husband and wife thing. Who knows?" But I really couldn't argue with her. It didn't sound right to me, either.

"Don't ask me. You're the one who was married."

"For all the good it did me."

"You said it, I didn't."

"Okay," I said, wanting badly to get off that topic, "but what about the $150,000?"

"You had Allie kind of cornered, Matt. Maybe she just wanted to avoid the humiliation of admitting to you that she and Kenny needed that kind of money, for whatever reason, and that she'd been turned down flat by David."

"You could be right, I guess. I never knew Allie all that well, so I guess I can't say one way or another."

"Right. And you're basically strangers now. I'm amazed that she told you as much as she did. She was bound to draw a line somewhere."

"Okay, but let's just for a minute assume that David did give her the $150 thousand. Where could he have gotten it from?"

"All I can tell you, Matt, is that Tommy Fornaio would have known if he'd gotten the money from anyone in his own territory. And I think your buddy Doreen has told you the truth. I mean, why would she lie to you?"

"I don't think she has. So where does that leave us?"

"In my mind, that leaves us with only two possibilities, assuming she actually did get the money: David somehow stole it from his wife and she doesn't know it yet. Or David got a loan from someone outside of Tommy's line of sight."

"I get the impression that Doreen's pretty sharp with money," I said, "so I'd discount the first possibility. I'll check with her, though, just in case."

"I'm sure you will," said Lacey.

"What's that supposed to mean?"

She stared at me for a long minute. "Nothing."

"So I guess that leaves us with the conclusion that David went somewhere else to get the money," I said, trying to get back on track. "Someplace that would be out of Tommy Fornaio's range."

"But where?" said Lacey. "He wasn't exactly a successful banker, so I doubt he had any banking connections he could rely on. And believe me, Tommy knows what goes on in New York City and the Tri-State area. I know he checked with his friends there."

"And David didn't have any close friends around here except Kenny. From what everybody's told me, he was kind of a hermit, except the charitable benefits he attended with Doreen. And I don't think he's been back to New York City since the day he graduated from NYU, so I don't know who he could have gone to there, especially that Tommy wouldn't have known about."

"You can't think of anyone else?" said Lacey.

"Lacey, I've been gone a long time."

"Then I guess you're going to have to ask Doreen."

"Oh, so now you *want* me to see Doreen?"

"Look, your personal life is none of my business, so let's not get into a spat about it. I'm sorry I ever brought it up."

"We're starting to sound like a couple of quarrelsome siblings, you know," I said, smiling.

"I guess it's a phase we missed when we were growing up," said Lacey, smiling back.

"We'll get over it," I said.

"Yeah, we will," said Lacey, perhaps ruefully.

"And you're not sorry you brought it up," I said, smiling again.

"Probably not," said Lacey. She stuck her tongue out at me.

"In the meantime," I said, trying hard not to laugh, "I owe my client an update, so I'd better get going."

"Yes, you should. You've been distracting me from my work long enough."

"Aw, c'mon, Lace. Admit it. You love this stuff."

"Ah, bullshit," she said. "Get out of here."

I gave her a hug on the way out. She hugged me back.

The rain had stopped, and I walked back to my car in the sunshine.

CHAPTER TWENTY-ONE

"T HAT'S JUST NOT POSSIBLE, MATT," said Doreen, pouring iced tea for both of us as we stood at her kitchen counter. The countertop was solid granite and, like the rest of the kitchen, reeked of the quality that only comes with an unlimited budget.

I should have called ahead, but I hadn't, and I'd apparently gotten to the house only a couple of minutes behind Doreen. She answered the door in a tennis outfit, and her face still looked flushed from the exercise. The skirt was really short, and the top was really tight.

"What do you mean?" I said, trying to remain focused.

"My money is kept in a brokerage account with J.P. Morgan. I am the only person who knows the password, and it also has a holographic image of both my hands, which must be confirmed before any transaction is executed. The only money David ever sees is the money I occasionally transfer into our checking account."

"So there's no way David could have hacked into it?"

"Nobody could, never mind David." She paused for a few seconds. "Just so you know, Matt, your sister designed the security software. Just about every major financial institution in the world uses it now."

"You're kidding," I said, feeling my jaw literally drop open.

"No, I'm not. You don't know much about your own sister, do you?"

"It seems I know less about everybody I thought I knew every time I wake up these days. But you're right, there's a lot about my sister I don't know."

"I didn't mean that as a criticism, Matt. There's a lot no one knows, and it's probably best that way. But what I do know is that your sister was, at one point in her life, the most notorious computer hacker in the world."

"*What?*"

"You heard me right," said Doreen. "The only way anyone ever knew they'd been hacked by her was that she announced herself every time she completed a successful hack. And before you get too upset, the other thing you need to know is that she never stole a penny or a single bit of personal information. Ever."

"Then why did she do it?"

"For the fun of it, as far as anyone could tell. And just to prove she could. She'd just leave little letter bombs at the sites she successfully hacked."

"What's a letter bomb?"

"It's just a term I made up, but it's just what it sounds like. For example, she once hacked into Jamie Dimon's personal account at J.P. Morgan." She must have seen my blank expression. "You don't know who that is, do you."

"Am I supposed to?" I said.

"It doesn't matter," she said. "All you need to know is that when she got into the account, she just left a little note that said, 'Have a nice day, Jamie!' and that was it. Everything else was left completely intact."

"Was she ever arrested?"

"The Feds wanted to," said Doreen, "but they didn't know her actual identity or where she was. And besides, the law back then was pretty vague, especially since she never stole anything. On top of that, what they really wanted, what everybody really wanted, was her expertise."

"So what happened?"

"What happened was that Lacey finally outed herself."

"Why?"

"Who knows?" said Doreen. "But my guess is that she got tired of the game, and she just wanted to get out of it. But I also think that she wanted people to know who she was."

"But why? Wasn't she just exposing herself to legal trouble?"

"Perhaps. But Lacey is a human being just like everyone else, and she has an ego."

"So what happened?" I asked.

"When the Feds finally found out who she was, they hired her to bolster their own security and, you know, our national security. They wanted her to design systems even she couldn't hack into. She told them the truth, which was that might be impossible, but that she'd design systems no one else in the world could hack into. They decided that was good enough, and she made a two-year exclusive commitment to them to avoid prosecution. When that was done, she went into private industry and made a fortune. She's as rich as I am."

"And is she still doing that?" I said, thinking of her monastic loft.

"No. The Feds hired her back. Even you must have read about all the hacks into government data systems by the Chinese and the Russians."

"Yes, I have. So what happened? Did the Chinese and the Russians beat Lacey at her own game?"

"No, they didn't. They just went around her."

"How did they do that?"

"As far as anybody can tell," said Doreen, "the Chinese played the race card and the Russians played the fear card."

"What does that mean?"

"Matt, there are hundreds of thousands of second and third generation, ethnically Chinese Americans in this country. They are native-born Americans just as you and I are, and are treated the same way you and I would be when it comes to security clearances. But the Chinese government has put tremendous pressure on them to realign their loyalties. They drill into them that no matter where they are, no matter what they do, they are first and foremost Chinese. They are told to think of themselves not as Chinese Americans, but as American-born Chinese. Then the Chinese government uses them for their own purposes."

"Aw, c'mon, Doreen," I said. "I know plenty of Chinese Americans. They're as American as I am. I just don't think they'd cave to that kind of pressure."

"You're right. Overwhelmingly, they don't. They think of themselves as Americans just as much as we do, and they are every bit as patriotic. But it only has to work once in a while, and once in a while, it does."

"And what about the Russians?"

"The Russians have never been famous for subtlety, Matt. As far as anyone can tell, they use the Russian mob to intimidate people. You know, when someone tells you that they're going to kidnap your kids and start chopping their limbs off, you'll do pretty much anything they tell you to do."

"So you're saying that they couldn't beat Lacey's security systems, so they just walked in the front door by turning employees at federal agencies?"

"That's most of it. But the other part is that they have just gotten awfully good at cyberattacks, and the techniques they're using now simply didn't exist when Lacey first designed her security systems."

"And it's tough to protect against something that doesn't even exist yet."

"Yes, it is. But if there's a way to do it, your sister will find it."

"Okay, I get it. But what I don't get is, if she's so rich, why does she live the way she does?"

"Because that's how she wants to live, for her own reasons. Just as I live the way I want to live, for my own reasons."

"I guess that's the definition of rich, isn't it," I said.

"Yes, it is," said Doreen. "Now, let's get back to business, shall we?"

"Yes, let's," I said.

"Leave your tea here," she said. "I don't like stuff that can spill around my computer." She put a hand on my upper arm and guided me out of the kitchen, down a hall, and up a stairway. We walked past what I assumed was her and David's bedroom to the next door in the hallway, and entered what was undoubtedly intended to be an extra bedroom, but which Doreen had converted into a spacious office. She sat down at a small but ergonomically efficient desk on which sat an enormous Apple iMac and began to tap keys. There was a large, framed photograph on the wall of David and Doreen and their wedding party. I had been the best man, and Kenny had been an usher. We all looked like children. I turned my attention back to Doreen, which wasn't difficult.

"What are you doing?" I said.

"I'm going to prove to both of us that David didn't steal any money from me," she said. "Grab a chair and sit down next to me."

I sat down to her left just as a thin, flat pad to the right of her computer lit up. She placed her right hand on it, palm down. There was a muted beep, and Doreen put her left hand on it. Almost instantaneously the computer screen lit up with a page filled with dates, account numbers and dollar figures. All of the account balances contained eight digits, some of them nine. There were charts with trendlines, all of which seemed to be moving up and to the right.

"What am I looking at?" I said.

"This is my portfolio," said Doreen, turning her mesmerizing eyes on me. "Stocks, bonds, precious metals, real estate. You know, the usual. Now, let's look at it this way."

She clicked on an icon. All the numbers shifted, but they were all still eight and nine figures.

"This displays all my activity in all my accounts for the past six months. As you can see, there has been almost none. I'm what you call a buy and hold kind of gal, you know?" she said, giving me a warm smile that bordered on sultry. Her face was close enough for me to kiss her if I'd had the nerve.

My brain sizzled. My pants started to feel tight. My mouth opened and closed, but nothing came out. She kept her eyes on me for a few seconds, and the smile lingered just long enough to let me know that she knew what she was doing to me.

"And, as you can also see," she said, abruptly turning back to the computer, "there have been no recent transactions for $150,000 or anything approaching that amount. I transferred a few thousand dollars into the joint checking account last month to cover normal living expenses. That's about it."

"Okay," I said, sitting back in my chair and trying not to think about the numbers I'd just seen, "you've convinced me that David didn't steal the money from you. So where do you think he might have gotten it?"

"I'm not at all sure he did."

"You mean, you think Allie was lying to me?"

"I think that's the most logical conclusion, Matt. I really can't think of anywhere else that David could've gotten that kind of money. He's just so naïve about financial matters."

"I'm sorry, Doreen," I said, "but you're going to have to explain something to me."

"What's that?"

"I know David wasn't as successful as I thought he was, but he still worked at a bank for almost twenty years. How could he be so ignorant about banking and money? I mean, something had to have rubbed off, right? And he had to have made at least some connections."

"Oh, Matt," said Doreen as she logged off the computer. When she turned to me the sultry smile was gone. "David works at a bank but he's not a banker."

"Then what is he?"

"He's what he's been all his life: David Chandler. When important clients come into the bank, especially ones who are from the local area, they parade David out for a meet and greet. He hands out autographed copies of that damned picture and regales them with tales of his heroics."

"Even after all these years, huh?"

"Yeah, but it's starting to get old. People are starting to forget. It isn't like he'd won the Super Bowl, you know?"

"So do you think his job is at risk?"

"Oh, Matt, I don't know. My only point was that he doesn't know anything about the world of finance because he really was never part of it, that's all. By the time any actual banking was transacted at those meetings he attended, David was long gone."

I found myself staring up at the wedding picture again, perhaps hoping it would keep me from fantasizing about Doreen minus the tennis outfit.

"It was a long time ago, wasn't it," she said, her eyes also focused on the photograph.

"Yeah, it was. Do you keep up with any of those folks?"

"I used to see my bridesmaids for weddings and baptisms, but that part of our lives is pretty much over now. I still see some of them occasionally, but that's about it."

"What about David?"

"No. Just Kenny, and you before you pulled the plug."

I kept staring at the picture. Something, something almost forgotten, was tickling my memory.

"What about his roommate?" I said, pointing at the only non-Caucasian person in the picture. "I can't remember his name now."

"You mean Peter?" said Doreen.

"That's right," I said. "Peter Kwan. They were roommates all four years at NYU, weren't they? I remember they were pretty tight."

"Yeah, they were," said Doreen. "I think he was the only close friend David made at college. David came home almost every weekend back then. He never got into the college social scene at all."

"Well, he was probably coming home to see you."

"No, he wasn't. I got as involved in college social life and student government every bit as much as I did in high school."

"So, what was he coming home for?"

"Just to be here, I guess. It never stopped being his comfort zone, still hasn't."

"Did he and Peter ever keep in touch with each other?"

"No, but it's funny you mentioned him. We just saw him about three months ago at a charity function. We had a nice chat. He's living out on Long Island with his wife, and I think he said two kids."

"How's he doing?"

"Apparently really well. He's running an import/export business."

"Weren't there rumors that his family was mixed up in organized crime down in Chinatown?"

"I guess I never heard that," said Doreen.

"Then it's probably something I heard when I was still a cop," I said.

"Matt, what are you thinking?" said Doreen, staring at me with widening eyes.

"I'm not sure yet."

"You're not thinking…"

"I know it's a stretch, Doreen. But right now it's all I've got."

"So, what are you going to do?"

"I've been away for a long time, but I've still got some connections at the NYPD. I think I'll make a few phone calls. Maybe somebody will still talk to me."

"I hate to say this, Matt, but this almost makes sense. I know Tommy Fornaio is well-connected, even in the five boroughs where he doesn't do any business, but I really doubt he has any connections in Chinatown."

"I hadn't thought about that, but you're right."

Doreen logged out of her accounts and shut down her computer. We left the office and headed back to the kitchen. The ice in our tea glasses had long since melted, but I took a drink from mine anyway.

"It's only three o'clock, Matt," said Doreen. "I'm going to get out of this sweaty tennis outfit and go for a swim. Do you want to keep me company? For that matter, you can stay for supper if you like. The kids are both going to be out late tonight." She looked at me, her eyes seemed to be inviting me to say "yes," but I knew that Lacey was right: I was probably just kidding myself. Or was I?

I don't understand women. I certainly didn't understand Doreen, no matter how badly I wanted to, no matter how much I wanted to believe that I wasn't just imagining the invitation in her eyes. I thought of the wedding picture, and I thought of my best friend. But I couldn't make myself stop wanting Doreen.

But in the end it wasn't guilt, it wasn't Lacey's admonitions that I was kidding myself, and it certainly wasn't a robust morality that saved me from myself.

It was Tommassino Fornaio, the thug, the man who had finally made me realize that what I really wanted, even more than I wanted Doreen, was not to be a mediocrity anymore. Tommassino Fornaio had forced me to confront the fact that I hadn't lived up to my own expectations or anyone else's since I'd taken off my football uniform for the last time, and I was sick to death of it. I'd been a good cop, and maybe I could have been the NYPD Police Commissioner; but I'll never know because I gave up on myself before anyone else gave up on me. Maybe I could have been a successful lawyer, but I was too sloppy and lazy to find out. I didn't even know how to file my own taxes, for chrissakes. No wonder Marianne dumped me. She was right: I was a failure, and I had no one but myself to blame for it.

And now I was pushing forty. I was running out of time. For once in my life, for nobody's sake but my own, I needed to devote myself to something, no matter what it was, and do it as well as it could be done. It didn't matter what I chose to do, it was how I chose to do it. That was the lesson I'd learned on the football field and had proceeded to forget as soon as I left it. I would never forget it again.

"Doreen," I heard myself say, as if from a distance, "you have no idea how much I'd love to stay, but I have to find David, and I have to find him before it's too late. I have to make a few phone calls before the day ends, and then I have to drive down to the city in the morning. I can't waste any more time. I hope you understand."

She was silent for a few seconds. She moved close to me and put her hand on my chest. She looked up at me with those eyes. She gave me a kiss that she let linger. So did I.

"I understand," she said, her eyes still boring into mine. "Maybe another time."

"Another time," I said.

I left while I still could.

CHAPTER TWENTY-TWO

SKIPPED THE THRUWAY AND TOOK THE PALISADES PARKWAY down to the Tappan Zee Bridge because it's such a pretty ride, especially on a summer morning. People used to call it "Harriman's Driveway," but no one remembers who Averell Harriman was anymore, so the nickname has lost its caché.

I spent most of the drive down thinking about Doreen, and that kiss. Until that moment, I'd been willing to listen to Lacey's lectures and assume that I was just kidding myself, that the attraction I felt for Doreen was a one-way street that led to a humiliating dead end, no matter what fantasies my loneliness was nudging me to engage in. But that kiss had been unmistakable: Doreen wanted me, too, and no one, including Lacey, could convince me otherwise. The question I should have been asking myself was, why? Of course, I now knew that a great deal of the David Chandler Persona was a fiction, and Doreen had been honest about that. But she had more than made up for any shortcomings he had as a provider, and she had never given me any indication that she was unhappy with the marriage because of his failures. Despite all that, she was genuinely worried about his disappearance, and she had paid me a lot of money to find him. And perhaps more than anything else, I knew Doreen Chandler; I'd grown up with her. She had an unbreakable moral compass. She just wouldn't behave like this. But she was, so what was I missing?

The drive went quickly. I'd waited until the rush hour was over, so the rest of the drive down to Manhattan was a slide on ice: The Saw Mill River Parkway to the Henry Hudson Parkway, down to 34th Street and over to the Midtown South Precinct House. Miraculously, there was a free parking space on 9th Avenue. I got out of my car and locked it, and my thoughts of Doreen were pushed to the back of my mind as I felt the soles of my shoes slap Manhattan pavement.

Walking into the NYPD precinct house was like walking into my old elementary school: Just the smell of it brought me back with a jolt to times long since past, memories long since buried, and to a self that I thought had ceased to exist. There's a rhythm to the place that I'd always loved, and it hurt to know that I was now just another outsider. I signed in at the front desk, and was escorted down a hallway by an attractive young patrolwoman who looked like she could kill me before I could say "good morning" if she'd been so inclined. She took me up the stairs to the Detectives' Squad Room, pointed to a cubicle in the far corner, and left without a word.

Walter Hudson and I were once patrolmen together, but he'd stuck to the path that I had always thought that I would take; he'd paid the price that I'd been unwilling to pay, and now he was a Detective Lieutenant. Follow-through is everything. Rumor had it that he was on an inside track to the Police Commissioner's office. I felt a twinge of jealousy that I had no right to feel as I walked into his small cubicle.

I'm a big man, but I'd always felt small next to Walter. He stood six-four in his bare feet and weighed two-forty, not an ounce of it fat. His massive head was covered with thick, dark hair, and his nose had been broken at least once. His hands were the size of cast iron frying pans, and just as hard. The man had landed a lot of punches in his life, and he had the swollen knuckles to show for it. I don't think I'd ever seen a man, no matter how tough, get up after being taken down by one of Walter's fists. But he had a boyish demeanor that was disarming, and the old joke had always been that the only human being on Earth that Walter Hudson feared was his tiny wife, Sarah.

I'd heard that Sarah had recently inherited a not-so-small fortune, but you'd never know it from looking at Walter. His dark, off-the-rack suit and his white shirt with a worn collar were clearly made of some synthetic blend, and his tie was frayed at the bottom.

"Matt, what a pleasant surprise!" he said, rising from his chair and offering me his hand. I managed not to wince.

"Thanks for seeing me on such short notice, Walter," I said. "You must be a busy man."

"Ah," he said, scanning his desk, "if you can call pushing paper being busy. I'd give up half my paycheck just to get back on a beat. Can I get you a cup of coffee?"

"Are they still lacing it with battery acid?" I said.

"Of course."

"Then I'll have a cup."

"How do you like it?"

"Black, please."

"Brave man," he said, as he walked off toward the coffee machine.

"So tell me again," said Walter, after he'd returned with two cups of coffee, "who this guy is you're looking for?"

"An old high school friend of mine," I said. "His wife hired me to find him."

"So you're a private dick now, huh?"

"That's the plan."

"I thought I heard you'd become a lawyer or something."

"I did, but it didn't work out the way I hoped it would."

"It usually doesn't," said Walter, grimacing. "I was never smart enough even to think about law school. Probably just as well."

"Trust me on that," I said, hoping to escape the conversation on a humorous note.

"And you think this guy, Peter Kwan, might know something?"

"I'm guessing, Walter. But David Chandler got a lot of money from someone, and this is the only lead I've got right now, so I'm chasing it down."

"I know the feeling," said Walter. The man was legendary for never giving up, chasing down every lead, and always closing his cases.

"I'm pretty sure Peter Kwan is on the up and up," I said, "but I've heard that his family might not be so much so."

"That's what I've heard, too," said Walter. "Look, Chinatown isn't my territory, and the Organized Crime Division usually handles stuff like this."

"So you think you could line me up with someone over there?"

"No," said Walter. "I mean, I could, but I won't."

"Oh," I said. A sinking feel started to settle in my stomach, and I didn't think it was the coffee.

"No, no, it's not that," said Walter, noticing my expression. "It's just that I don't think you want to hook yourself up with those guys."

"Why not?"

"The Organized Crime guys are in their own little world, you know? They don't like interlopers, not even guys like me. And besides, if they did agree to help you, they'd be fitting you for bugs, giving you a crash course on how not to sweat too much, and otherwise taking your measurements for a coffin. I don't think that's the kind of help you want."

"No, it's not," I said.

"So anyway, I didn't want you to leave here empty-handed, so I asked a friend to stop by." Just as he finished speaking his eyes shifted toward the door and a smile lit up his face. "Levi!" he said. "Come on in." He turned to me and said, "Matt, I'd like you to meet Levi Welles, NYPD's new Deputy Commissioner for Intelligence."

So this is Leviticus Welles, I thought to myself, a man already a legend in his own time. Just a few years back, the story went, he'd been an unemployed salesman, but then he'd stumbled on a dying man in an alley near the Empire State Building. He'd helped then Sergeant Walter Hudson tug ever so patiently on the loose threads of that murder until they eventually unraveled what could have been one of the most disastrous conspiracies in the history of the nation. Police Commissioner Sean Donahue had noticed, and the rest, as they say, is history.

He was an unprepossessing man of average height with a slight build, and his close-cropped hair was thinning and going silver at the fringes. He wore gold-rimmed glasses that magnified his eyes, giving him a bookish appearance. I guessed he was about fifty.

"Levi," said Walter, "this is Matt Hunter, an old friend of mine. He's an ex-NYPD beat cop, so you know you can't trust him."

"Nice to meet you," said Levi reaching out his hand to shake mine. It was half the size of Walter's, but it was dry and his grip was firm. His voice was soft, and conveyed genuine warmth.

"It's a pleasure to meet you, sir," I said.

"Please, it's Levi," he said.

"Coffee, Levi?" said Walter.

"Uh, thanks, but no," said Levi. The two exchanged grins.

"So, Matt," said Walter, "why don't you tell Levi your story."

I probably talked for about five minutes, going back to the beginning of my involvement in the case and my background with David and Doreen. Levi listened quietly, his eyes alert behind the glasses. He took no notes and asked no questions.

"Interesting story," said Levi after I'd finished. "Mixing your personal life with your business always makes things messy. Believe me, I know, and so does Walter." Walter nodded emphatically.

"It's not something I'll ever do again," I said.

"Oh, you probably will," said Levi, "but at least you'll know what you're getting yourself into next time."

"So, what can you tell us about the Kwans, Levi?" said Walter.

"Not much, but I think what we do know might fit with your case." He had brought no notes with him, and he kept his eyes steadily on me while he spoke. "Peter Kwan, in fact, runs a successful import/export business, named South China Commerce, Ltd. The business is run out of a warehouse in Long Island City, but Peter rents office space in the Empire State Building where he maintains an office staff and meets with customers."

"Thereby giving me a cover for sticking my nose into this in case if anyone asks, since the Empire State Building is in my precinct," said Walter.

"Right," said Levi. "In any event, he seems to be respected in the industry and lives a quiet life with his wife and two kids out on Long Island. He's not rich, but he seems to be doing well enough."

"What about his family?" I said.

"His father died young of apparently natural causes, but who knows? Young Peter was brought up by his mother, his grandmother, and his paternal grandfather, Alistair Kwan."

"Alistair?" I said. "Is that his real name?"

"Well, he has a Chinese name, of course, but Alistair is what he goes by. The old man is in his eighties now, but he apparently still runs a large organized crime operation in Chinatown. He's supposedly immensely wealthy, but he still lives with his wife in the little apartment on Mott Street where they raised Peter. His wife still cooks all his meals for him."

"What kinds of activities is he into?"

"You name it: human trafficking; prostitution; drugs; gambling, and, of course, loansharking."

"I'm assuming at reasonable rates," I said.

"The best information we have is thirty to one hundred percent per month, but it's hard to get people to talk about it. The ones who do talk are often already missing a few fingers or a hand, and they usually turn up dead afterwards."

"Do you think Peter Kwan would have referred his friend to his grandfather?" I said. "Why not just loan him the money personally?"

"Because his grandfather's strictest rule is that Peter can never even give the appearance of being involved in his businesses. Peter must be immaculate in the eyes of the law."

"And is he?"

"Well, we strongly suspect that Granddad uses Peter's business to launder his money, but no one can prove it."

"Still," I said, "I think it's odd that Peter would send a friend into the warm embrace of Granddad."

"I imagine your friend David insisted," said Levi. "It sounds like he was desperate."

"So, where do I go from here?" I said.

"I would suggest," said Levi, "that you call Peter and see if he'll talk to you. I'm pretty sure, though, that he's going to send you to see his grandfather."

"And at that point," said Walter, "you call me. Do not, I repeat, do not go down to Chinatown alone. Do you understand?"

"I think I do," I said.

"Good," said Detective Lieutenant Walter Hudson.

CHAPTER TWENTY-THREE

'D LIVED AND WORKED IN NEW YORK CITY for years, but I'd never been inside the Empire State Building. It's a New Yorker thing. Tourists go to the Statue of Liberty, take the Circle Line, and take the elevator all the way to the top of the Empire State Building. New Yorkers don't.

The offices of South China Trading Company, Ltd., Peter Kwan, President, were on the 37th floor, so I took the elevator to the 37th floor. The offices occupied a large corner space that stared out at the United Nations building to the east and Central Park to the north. Peter Kwan occupied the corner office.

He hadn't changed a lot since the last time I'd seen him at Doreen and David's wedding. He was still slim in a nicely tailored suit, still had a thick head of dark, carefully combed hair, and his face was tanned and unlined. Long Island living clearly suited him.

"It's good to see you again, Matt," he said as he shook my hand, smiling. His teeth were white and even. "It's been a long time."

He'd sounded hesitant to talk to me when I'd called. I think he remembered that I'd been headed to the NYPD after college, but even after I'd managed to convey at the beginning of the conversation that I'd long since left the force he'd still sounded cautious. He sounded friendly enough now, though. I'd actually been more than a little surprised when he agreed to see me. But then he must have figured that he would immediately arouse any suspicions I had if he refused; so he probably decided to take his chances on the hope that he could deflect me and, most importantly, keep me away from his grandfather. I tried to remind myself that it was still possible that he had nothing to do with David Chandler's mysterious money, even though every cop instinct in my body told me that he did. Either way, I was now going to find out.

"Yes, it has," I said. "It's good to see you, too."

"I was just about to have some tea. Would you like some?"

"That sounds great," I said, not lying. The precinct house coffee had gone down hard.

He pushed a button on an intercom and said, "Nancy, could you please bring us some tea? Thanks."

Peter invited me over to a corner furnished with a comfortable looking sofa, a couple of chairs, and a coffee table. Before we'd even had a chance to get settled, an attractive middle-aged Caucasian woman, presumably Nancy, came bearing a large tray with a pot of hot water, a creamer, a bowl of sugar, and two mugs, each with a paper tag that said "Lipton Tea" hanging over the rim. She set it on the table and left. So much for the mysterious Orient. We each poured our tea. I added cream; Kwan didn't.

"So, you told me on the phone that you wanted to talk about David Chandler," said Kwan. "What is it in particular that you'd like to discuss?"

"David has been missing for almost two weeks now, Peter. His wife and I suspect it may have something to do with money. I know that you saw both David and Doreen at a social function earlier this year, and I was wondering if he had approached you, either at that time or subsequently, regarding a loan."

"David and I are not close, Matt. That is the only time I've seen either him or his wife since their wedding."

"But you were close once, close enough to be a member of his wedding party. If he were in big enough trouble, I wouldn't be surprised if he came to you, especially since he'd just bumped into you at a social event."

"Look, I feel bad for the both of them, but why would he approach me?"

"Because you are one of his oldest friends, and you are apparently successful. David was probably pretty desperate."

"I am successful, but I am not rich, Matt. Life on the North Shore of Long Island is expensive, and both my children are in private schools. Even if he had come to me, I am hardly in a position to loan someone I haven't seen in almost twenty years $150,000."

"Who said anything about $150,000?"

"I thought you mentioned that sum," said Kwan, reddening.

I'd gotten the lucky break I so desperately needed. I wasn't surprised. Peter Kwan was an amateur, playing a game he had no business playing. I drained my teacup and put it back on the tray. The Lipton tea was actually pretty good.

"Let's cut the crap, okay?" I said. "David Chandler came to you in desperation and asked you to lend him $150,000. What did you tell him?"

"Perhaps he did, and perhaps he didn't," said Kwan, just making things worse for himself. "But if he did, it was a private matter between him and me. I see no reason to discuss it with you."

"Mr. Kwan – Peter - the man is missing. I can't even be sure that he's still alive, and his wife, a woman you know, is frantic. I understand your desire to keep your business transactions private, and under normal circumstances I would completely respect that. But these are not normal circumstances."

"Mr. Hunter, you have to understand that this goes beyond David and me. I have other things that I must take into consideration. Other people."

"I hope you understand that it isn't my job to worry about your other considerations."

"But I have to worry about them just the same, Mr. Hunter."

I was getting nowhere.

"I haven't lost all my connections in law enforcement, Peter." I didn't know how much I even believed that. Lieutenant Hudson and Deputy Commissioner Welles had both been polite and helpful to me to an extent, but I had no idea how much more help they'd be willing to give me.

He stared at me hard for a long time. He refilled our teacups, which we both ignored. He was buying time.

"Mr. Kwan?"

"Okay," he said, finally. "Yes, David Chandler came to me and asked me to lend him the money."

"And what did you tell him?"

"I told him just what I told you, that I wasn't in a position to lend him that kind of money; and even if I was, it is my strict personal rule not to be involved, ever, in that kind of business."

"Is that your rule or your grandfather's rule?"

"You would be well-advised to keep my grandfather out of this discussion," said Peter, with a hint of fear in his voice.

"I don't think I can do that, Peter. I know that your grandfather is involved, heavily involved, in the, ah, private banking business."

"You can think what you want, Matt, but the plain fact is that I am in no way involved in my grandfather's business dealings. I never have been, and I never will be, and I know nothing about them. That is his rule as well as mine, and we never break it."

"I don't doubt that, but that wouldn't stop you from making a referral."

"I don't make referrals."

"Not even for your old college roommate, when he was clearly in some kind of serious trouble?"

"I told David in no uncertain terms that he should make every effort to find another source for the money he needed."

"And what did he say?"

"He said he'd already done that."

"And then what did you say?"

"Matt, please."

"Did you refer David Chandler to your grandfather?"

"Please, Matt, leave this alone."

"Did you?"

"Okay, okay," said Peter, the fear in his voice creeping into his eyes. "No, I did not make a referral to my grandfather. I did make a call, however, to one of my grandfather's business associates, an attorney who specializes in financial matters."

"I'd like his name and address, please."

"Are you sure about this, Matt?" said Kwan. "I am asking this for your own sake, not mine."

"I can take care of myself," I said, pretty much positive that I didn't believe it. But once you're in up to your waist, you might as well get in up to your neck; and in up to my neck was where I was going to be if I started messing with Granddad Kwan's colleagues. But there was no turning back now.

He gave me another long look that said he wasn't so sure about it either. Then, without a word, he walked over to his desk, tore off a sheet of paper from a memo pad and jotted something on it with a fountain pen. He walked over and handed it to me. It contained an address on Pine Street, downtown in the financial district, and a phone number.

"No name?" I said.

"I'll call ahead. They'll be expecting you in about an hour, so you'd better hurry. And Mr. Hunter, please listen carefully: I don't ever want to see you again. I don't ever want to talk to you again. Whatever you do, and whatever may happen to you, is none of my concern. Do you understand, Mr. Hunter?"

"I understand," I said, feeling a droplet of sweat trickle down my back.

"Good."

"I only have one more question," I said. He ignored me, but I asked him anyway. "Peter, do you have any idea where David Chandler might be hiding, assuming he's still alive?"

Peter Kwan returned to his desk and sat down. He began to peruse some documents and made no attempt to make any eye contact with me. I presumed I was dismissed.

I left the office and got back on the elevator. It was crowded with tourists coming back from the Observation deck. I wished I was one of them. I took it to the ground floor and left the building. I didn't look up, and I didn't look back.

CHAPTER TWENTY-FOUR

"**N**OT EXACTLY WHAT YOU EXPECTED, MR. HUNTER?" said the stunning blonde, with a slight accent that I couldn't place, as she came around from behind her desk and shook my hand. The nameplate on the desk said that she was "Daria Evanishyn, President." She was tiny; she walked like a ballerina, and she had perhaps the most spectacular blue eyes I'd ever seen. Her smile revealed slightly crooked teeth that only added to her allure.

The address that Peter Kwan had written down had said only "37 Pine Street, Suite 3C." I'd contacted Lieutenant Hudson as soon as I left Kwan's office, and he'd met me outside the Empire State Building in an unmarked squad car driven by the same young patrolwoman who had escorted me to his office. She drove like a pro, and we made our way downtown in no time. Hudson got out with me, but he said he'd wait in the lobby while I did my business. That was fine with me, but it was nice knowing that I had backup a quick phone call away.

According to the occupant listing in the lobby, Suite 3C was occupied by a company called "Odessa Financial Advisors." I guess if I'd been a really good detective the "Odessa" part would have been an important clue.

"I'm sorry, I guess I didn't know what to expect," I said.

"Of course you did," she said, dazzling me with another smile as she retook her seat behind her desk and motioned me to a chair on the opposite side. I didn't know how many more of those smiles I could take before I offered her my hand in marriage. "You were expecting an old Chinese man."

"Okay," I said, seeing no sense in denying it, "that was exactly what I was expecting, Ms... Ms. Evan-"

"Evanishyn," she said, giving the final vowel an odd twist that I knew I couldn't mimic. "My name is Daria Evanishyn. Please call me Daria."

"So you're Russian, Daria."

"Oh, Mr. Hunter, let's not get off on the wrong foot. I am Ukrainian by birth, but now I am a proud American citizen. I got my undergraduate degree from Dartmouth and my M.B.A. and J.D. from Harvard."

"Well, don't I feel stupid."

"Please don't. It's a common mistake."

"I don't mean to be nosey, but how did a firm like yours come to work for a man like Alistair Kwan?"

"I wouldn't exactly characterize it as 'working for,' Mr. Hunter," said Daria. "I would say that we are... associates."

"Okay, then," I said. "Then how did you become associated with Alistair Kwan? I'd always thought that the Chinese, uh, business community, kept to itself. And please, call me Matt."

"Alistair Kwan is a visionary, Matt, and we came to admire his business acumen. So we reached out to him and described our business model and expansion plans. He quickly saw the advantages of associating with us instead of competing with us, especially since his son was dead and his grandson was not part of his succession plan."

"Who's 'we'?"

"Oh, please, Matt. You are surely not that naïve."

I was, but I was catching on quickly. I decided to move on.

"You're right," I said, "and I'm wasting your time."

"I am at your disposal, Matt. But I'm sure you don't want to leave your colleague, Lieutenant Hudson, cooling his heels down in the lobby for too long. I'm sure he's a busy man."

Daria Evanishyn was impressing me more by the minute.

"Yes, he is."

"I presume you understand the necessity for this conversation to be private."

"I think I do."

"Good, then I hope you won't mind if one of my colleagues confirms that you are not wearing any recording devices?"

"Of course not." So it was going to be like that.

As if on cue, a tall, stocky, bullet-headed man with thinning brown hair and an unhealthy complexion entered the office. The privacy of our conversation was apparently a one-sided proposition. He quickly and professionally patted me down, gave Daria a nod, and left the office without saying a word.

"Good," she said. "Now, how may I help you?"

"An old friend of mine, David Chandler, was in bad need of some money. He went to his former college roommate, Peter Kwan, for help. Apparently Peter Kwan referred him to you."

"Yes," said Daria, pursing her lips, "Peter made a bad mistake in judgment, and now he's made another one. Both his grandfather and we have firmly agreed that Peter is not to be involved in our business partnership in any way. I can assure you that his grandfather has already spoken to him, and now he will speak to him again. For his sake, I hope he listens this time. But what's done is done, and here we are. So, yes, David Chandler came to me and requested a loan of $150,000."

"And you gave it to him?"

"Normally, we wouldn't deal in sums so inconsequential, but because Peter so sentimentally inserted himself into the situation, we felt that we had no choice but to honor his request."

"So you loaned him $150,000?"

"Yes, we did."

"And what were the terms?"

"The loan is repayable in full on August 15th, exactly two months after he received the funds."

"And I'm sure there was interest attached to the loan?"

"Yes, we offered David our preferred customer rate of 50 percent per month, so the amount due on August 15th will be $337, 500." In David's defense, he probably hadn't understood the interest factor, at least not until it was bluntly explained to him after he had already received the money.

"My God. What's your non-preferred customer rate?"

"Actually, that's none of your business, but it's 50 percent per week."

"No wonder David disappeared."

"As you can imagine, we were quite concerned to learn of David's disappearance."

"How did you find out about it?" I said.

"We follow up with our newer customers on a regular basis. The last time we tried to touch base with him, he couldn't be found."

"Of course," I replied. That explained the disappearance. I could only imagine how friendly the follow-up calls must have been, and how frightened David must have become once he realized the full magnitude of what he had gotten himself into.

"Peter's grandfather insisted that Peter guarantee the loan, but, because he's a family member, he will only be obliged to repay the principal, and we will make no money on the transaction. That is bad business all around. Which brings us back to you, doesn't it?"

"I'm sorry? I'm not following."

"Yes you are, Matt," said Daria, giving me a smile that was suddenly chilly. "You are clearly a loyal friend. We know you and David grew up together, and that you also appear to be close to his wife. So we think it's only reasonable, in the unlikely event that Mr. Chandler defaults on his obligation, to expect you to step into his shoes and repay your friend's loan for him, interest included, of course."

It wasn't like this surprised me. I'd never worked in the Organized Crime division, but you can't be an NYPD cop without understanding how these people operate. I wasn't concerned because I'd seen Doreen's financial statements, and I knew she'd make good on the loan if she had to. But, for Doreen's sake, I didn't want the lovely Daria even to suspect any of that.

"But I don't have that kind of money! For God's sake, I'm broke!" I said, making my debut as an actor. I hoped it was convincing.

"That is not our concern, Matt. Why do you think we agreed to see you? Out of the kindness of our hearts? Out of genuine concern for David Chandler? Please. I know you're smarter than that."

"I'm just telling you that I have no way of repaying that kind of money."

"The interest and principal are repayable on August 15, Matt," said Daria, in a businesslike tone. "We don't really care who repays it. But please be aware, our default terms are harsh."

"What does that mean?"

"I don't think you need to ask. You were a cop."

"You're right. I don't think I do."

"Then I think our business is concluded."

"Yes, it is," I said. "I got what I came for."

"And so did we," said Daria.

We shook hands as if we'd just closed a deal on a used car, and she gave me another one of her dazzling smiles as I turned to leave, but somehow the charm had gone out of it.

******

"I guess you could say New York's a dynamic place, Matt," said Lieutenant Hudson, as we walked down Pine Street toward the unmarked car that was waiting for us. "The Chinese moved in and shoved the Italians out of the way, and now the Russians and Ukrainians are moving in and shoving everyone out of the way."

"They're a tough bunch, huh?"

"The toughest. You don't want to know. So if I were you, I'd find your friend David pretty damn quick or hope to win Powerball." I liked Walter Hudson, and I trusted him implicitly, but there had been no need to tell him about Doreen.

"So you think she was serious about me guaranteeing the loan?"

"These people are never not serious. I'm sorry Matt; I should have seen this coming and steered you away from ever getting involved in a mess like this."

"Don't worry, Walter; I would have gone to see Peter Kwan with your help or without it. It's my job."

Walter glanced over at me with something approaching admiration, and it made me feel good.

We were only a few yards from the car when a man came up behind Hudson and jostled him. I looked around and immediately recognized the bullet-headed guy who had patted me down in Daria's office.

"Careful there, sport," said Hudson.

"No, you and your friend be careful, sport," said the guy with a thick accent that told me he was a recent arrival to our fair shores.

"What are you talking about?" said Hudson, turning to look at the guy without breaking his stride.

"Walter," I said, "I met this guy at the office just now."

"Yes, Mr. Hunter," said the guy. "And it better be the last time we meet, because the next time will not go so well. Do you understand?"

"I understand," I said.

"And that goes for you and your fucking NYPD, too," he said, jostling Hudson again. "This is none of your fucking business."

I never really saw what happened next. I thought I saw Hudson raise his arm and make something like a flicking motion, but I really couldn't be sure. In the next instant the bullet-headed guy dropped to the sidewalk like he'd been shot. His face bounced hard off the pavement. One of his legs gave a twitch, and then he was still. Hudson kept walking.

"I'm sorry, Walter," I said. "I'm sure this isn't how you wanted to spend your day."

"Every day's a great day to be a cop, Matt," was all he said, smiling as we got into the car.

He was still smiling as the car pulled away from the curb, and he was still smiling as he stared at the bullet headed guy still lying motionless on the sidewalk as we drove by.

But I knew he was going to get up off the pavement sooner or later, and when he did, I was going to have to be careful. Enforcers live and die by their reputations, and he would have to get revenge, or the sharks would come out and the blood in the water would be his.

I looked over at Lieutenant Hudson, the man who had taken him down before he even knew what hit him, the man with the full force and authority of the NYPD behind him. I didn't think the guy would seek his revenge against him.

I was going to have to be very careful.

CHAPTER TWENTY-FIVE

"**N**O WONDER YOU WERE SO TIRED," said Doreen. "What the hell has David gotten himself into?"

"That's a damn good question," I said.

We were sitting on the banged up sofa in my tiny living room drinking coffee. I'd planned to go directly over to her house after I'd gotten back from the city the night before, but I was more exhausted than I'd realized. So I'd picked up a pizza and a six-pack on the way home, drove straight back to the duplex, and turned on the Mets game. I fell asleep in the fifth inning after only three slices of pizza and two beers, and that's how Doreen had found me at eight the following morning after she'd driven over because she couldn't get me to answer my cell phone. The battery had apparently died on the way back from the city, but I'd been too tired to notice. I was still clutching my beer, and I hadn't spilled a drop. At least I had my pants on.

I'd run upstairs to brush my teeth and splash some water on my face while she put the rest of the pizza in the fridge and made some coffee.

"I just don't understand it," she said. "If he really needed the money that badly, he should've just told me."

"Well, like you said, he really doesn't have any idea how much you're worth. Maybe he just believed that you didn't have it."

"Maybe, but that doesn't explain why he was so desperate that he went to a bunch of homicidal hoods to get it."

"Maybe he just didn't want to let Kenny down. If he really believed Allie that Kenny had gotten himself in trouble gambling, maybe he thought he had to protect him."

"What, and put himself in the same predicament?"

"Well, yes," I said. "Maybe it's just part of the David Chandler Legend, you know? The guy who could always come up with the right play when the team needed it the most. And if he's as bad with money as you say he is, he probably didn't realize what he'd gotten himself into until it was too late."

"Perhaps," said Doreen, but she sounded dubious.

"By the way," I said, "how'd the Mets do?"

"5-2."

"I guess I don't need to ask."

"No, you don't."

The front door flew open without a knock, and Lacey walked in. She was wearing a threadbare pair of khakis with a tear in the right knee and a "Dire Straits 'Money For Nothing' Tour" tee shirt that hung on her thin frame.

"Hi guys," she said, heading straight for the kitchen. I heard the refrigerator door open and bang close and some rustling noises, and she soon reappeared with the box containing the left over two-thirds of my large pizza and a Styrofoam McDonald's coffee cup.

"Jeez, Lace," I said, "that McDonald's cup has been in the garbage since yesterday morning."

"It's not the first time in my life I've gone dumpster diving, bro. And perhaps if you'd get a couple more coffee cups I wouldn't have to upset your delicate sensibilities."

"I've got about a hundred mugs at home, Matt," said Doreen. "I'll bring a few over next time I stop by."

"Thanks," said Lacey. "Otherwise we'll have to wait until the Mets win another World Series."

"Wiseass," I said.

"Anyone want a slice of pizza?" said Lacey, sitting down and opening the box.

"No, thanks," Doreen said.

"I'll pass for now," I said.

"Good," said Lacey, diving in. "So, what's up?"

I told her what I'd already told Doreen, and added in the fact that I was now on the hook for the repayment.

"Matt, that's terrible!" said Doreen.

Lacey laughed out loud.

"What's so damn funny?" I said.

"You haven't made that much money in your entire life, Matt. What the hell were you thinking about?"

"It's not like I volunteered, Lace."

"Matt, I'm going to take care of that, and I'm going to do it right away," said Doreen.

"How are you going to do that?" I said.

"I'm going to get a cashier's check written for the entire amount, and you're going to get it to your old buddy, Walter Hudson. Hopefully, he won't mind walking it over to the Empire State Building and handing it to Peter Kwan."

Lacey gave Doreen a contemplative stare, but said nothing.

There was a knock on the door, but before I could get up from the sofa the door opened, and Marianne Boulanger Hunter, of all people, walked in. Judging from the look on her face, she wasn't here just to see how I was doing.

******

"Well, well," she said, glaring at Doreen and me. "This didn't take long, did it?"

She was the last person I wanted to see, especially with Doreen practically sitting on my lap on the small sofa, but at least she'd knocked.

Marianne was born and raised in Greenwich, Connecticut, but I'd met her in a bar in Manhattan, where she'd been studying economics at Columbia at the same time I was at John Jay. She'd been pretty in that Fairfield County kind of way, but I'd convinced myself that I'd been attracted more to her intellect than her looks. Looking back, I think what I'd been attracted to had been the sure sense of purpose that she had so strongly emanated, even back then, and that I had so completely lacked. But a mistake was a mistake, and it was no more apparent than now.

"Give it a break, Marianne," I said. She was still pretty, I guess. A pair of sunglasses sat atop her perfectly coiffed brunette hair that now sported streaks of blond. She had nice eyes that she knew how to make up for maximum effect. But the thin, pursed lips ruined the effect, and her once kind of nice little body was now fashionably starved. Even without the past, I'm not sure I would have found her attractive anymore.

"And if it isn't dear, sweet little Lacey. What a pleasant surprise."

"Bite me, Marianne."

"That's about what I'd expect from you," said Marianne. "You can take the girl out of the gutter, but you can't take the gutter out of the girl, can you?"

"Just sayin', Marianne," said Lacey, with a smile on her face. "Bite me." She went back to her pizza.

"Enough," I said. "Look, Marianne, Doreen's here because David's gone missing, and she's hired me to find him."

"She mustn't be too anxious to find him, then," said Marianne. "But how lovely for you."

"Okay, Marianne," I said. "You've made your point. You're still the biggest bitch I've ever met in my life. We can retire the trophy, okay? You win. But I'm sure you didn't come here just so we could exchange pleasantries. What do you want?"

"You clearly don't have anything I want," she said, looking around the room.

"Well, since nobody here gives Botox treatments or does boob jobs, you're probably right," said Lacey.

"Why, you little slut…"

"Just sayin', Marianne. Something to think about."

I couldn't help it; I burst out laughing. Marianne's face reddened and looked like it was going to explode, and her whole body seemed to quiver. The only thing Marianne hated more than losing a verbal joust was losing one while I was there to watch. I almost started to feel bad for her.

"Marianne," I said. "Please tell me what you came here for and then leave. Please."

It took her a couple of tries to unsnap her large bag because her hands were shaking, but she finally succeeded. She reached in and pulled out an envelope.

"Here," she said, holding the envelope out to me without moving.

I got up and walked toward her just far enough to take the envelope from her and sat back down next to Doreen, who hadn't spoken a word since Marianne had walked in the door.

"What's this?" I said.

"It's a check for $10,000, representing our final settlement, and two copies of the final divorce papers: the original for you to sign and one for you to keep. Take your time reviewing the documents and just mail the signed original to my lawyer when you're done." She seemed to be rapidly regaining her composure. I'd always admired her resilience.

"You drove all the way over here, unannounced, just to hand this stuff to me?" I said. "You could've just mailed it."

"No, this is something I wanted to get done as soon as possible."

"And you wanted to get a first-hand look at just how badly I was doing, right?"

"I'm too busy for that kind of petty nonsense."

"Hah," said Lacey, through a mouthful of pizza.

"You got a pen in that purse?" I said, opening the envelope.

"Of course I do."

"May I borrow it please?"

She reached into her purse, withdrew the pen, and actually took a step toward me, just close enough so that I could reach out and take the pen from her. I pulled the documents out of the envelope and spread them on the coffee table, careful to avoid a greasy spot where a stray piece of melted mozzarella had dropped on it the night before. I jotted a note on the original of the divorce settlement, signed the document, initialed the note, and handed it back to my ex-wife along with the check.

"Don't forget to initial the note," I said.

"Matt," she said, holding the check back out to me, "this check is yours. It's part of the settlement you just signed. If you don't take it my lawyer will have to redraft the settlement."

"I don't want it, and it's no longer part of the settlement as soon as you initial the note I just wrote."

She looked at the document, and I saw her eyes scan the note, which said, "$10,000 settlement amount reduced to $0 in return for valuable consideration."

"I don't understand," she said. "What's the 'valuable consideration'?"

"Oh, I think we both know what that is," I said, walking to the door and opening it. "I think we're done here, don't you?"

And then Marianne Boulanger Hunter did the single most surprising thing I'd ever seen her do in all the years I'd known her.

She burst into tears.

"Marianne…"

"Just shut up, okay?" she said. She stuffed the settlement and the check back in her purse and left without another word.

"I think that went well, don't you?" said Lacey as she polished off the last slice of pizza.

And then Doreen burst into tears.

"I'm sorry you had to see that, Doreen," I said.

"Shut up, Matt," she said, rising from the sofa and heading for the door.

"Doreen, I…"

"You men don't understand anything, do you?" she said, glaring at me. She turned and left, banging the door behind her.

I turned to Lacey and said, "What was that all about?"

"You've got a lot to learn, Matt," she said as she dropped the empty pizza box on the coffee table and headed for the door.

"Where are *you* going?" I said.

"Show's over and the pizza's gone. I'm outta here," she said as she slipped her slender frame out the door.

I stood in the middle of the room and stared at the door for a long time. Then I went back to the kitchen to pour myself another cup of coffee, but the pot was empty. I slammed it back onto the counter and stared at it.

"Fuck it," I said.

Then I walked out the door, too.

CHAPTER TWENTY-SIX

HEADED OVER TO MICKEY D'S for some comfort food, but by the time I got there I realized that I was too fed up to have an appetite, so I went back home, put on a pair of running shorts and an old Mets tee shirt, and drove over to the high school to go for a run.

The old high school track had gone the way of the old football field. Cinders had been replaced by an artificial surface that had a cushiony feel to it, and the circumference was now 400 meters instead of 440 yards. I had to admit, though, that the new surface felt good to my complaining knees. I remembered when David and I were kids how we'd competed with each other to see who could be the first to run a mile in under five minutes. I looked down at my watch now and realized I was barely running at an eight-minute pace, and my legs felt heavy.

I'd only run a couple of miles when I saw five high school-aged kids jogging over to the football field. One of the kids was carrying a football, and I immediately recognized him as Kenny Cooper, Junior. He was laughing and loping in an effortless way that made me jealous.

He didn't resemble his father much physically. Kenny Senior had always been a mesomorph, with a broad chest, bulging arms, and thick thighs. His son was well built, but his physique was much more like mine had been as a kid: built more for speed than for running over defending linemen. It was a build he'd gotten from his mother's side of the family, I thought. I vaguely recalled that Allie's brother had been a damn good athlete himself. The apple never falls far from the tree.

As he ran by me he called out, "Hey, you're Matt Hunter!" He slowed down.

It was good to have an excuse to stop running, if that was what you could call it. I walked over to him and shook his hand.

"And you must be Kenny Junior."

"Chip off the old block, huh?" he said, smiling easily.

"Yeah, you're tough to miss," I said, even though he didn't look like his father at all. He had his mother's dark coloring, and her nose. He was a good-looking kid.

"My Dad talks about you all the time. He says you had the best pair of hands he'd ever seen."

"Catching the ball is easy when you've got a good quarterback throwing to you."

"But you still gotta have the hands. Hey! Guys! This is Matt Hunter. You know, the third guy in that picture." They all came over, and we shook hands all around to a chorus of deep-throated "Hey's."

"So, hey, Mr. Hunter, do you want to run a few routes?" said Kenny. "These guys are all a bunch of pussies and they say I throw the ball too hard."

"Shit, Kenny," said one. "I still got a bruise the size of a softball from the last pass I caught." To prove his point, he lifted up his tee shirt. The bruise was just starting to turn color and it was a beauty.

"You sure you didn't crack one of those ribs?" I said.

"Yeah, I had it checked out," said the kid. "It'll be okay."

"So, will ya?" said Kenny.

"Why not?" I said. It was tough to back down at that point, and besides, I was curious. I jogged about twenty yards down the field and turned around.

"Somebody better call an ambulance," I heard one of the kids joke as they sat down on the field to watch the show.

"Just a couple of soft tosses first," I said, "and then I'll run a few routes, okay?"

"Okay," said Kenny.

"*Okay*," said one of the other guys. The others chuckled.

Kenny tossed the ball to me with a motion so smooth it looked almost lazy, so I was shocked when the ball came hissing at me like an angry rattlesnake. I got my hands up just in time, but the ball left my fingers tingling. I'd done this before, and it felt good to be doing it again, despite the sting. He made a few more practice tosses and then I jogged back to him. I heard the other guys murmuring something.

"Okay," I said, "let's start out with a little down and out. I'll break right at about twenty yards."

Kenny nodded. I lined up beside him and heard him give a soft, "hut." I took off and made a nice, clean cut twenty yards downfield. I looked back, trying to look smooth, but the ball was already on top of me. It was only the years of doing this with David that saved me. I got my hands up and I hoped I made it look easy, but my hands were on fire.

"Okay," I said when I got back. "How about a little button route, same distance."

Kenny nodded and I lined up again.

"Hut."

It was the same thing. I was a little better prepared this time, but still, the ball got by my hands a little and I felt a rib go numb. I tried not to let it show.

As I jogged back I noticed that the peanut gallery had quieted down considerably.

Then we ran a crossing pattern. At least on a crossing pattern I was able to keep my eyes on Kenny as I ran my route. I saw him as he dropped back, his footwork perfect, and let the ball go with that easy motion. The ball came at me so fast he only had to lead me by a foot or two. I never had to break my stride, and the ball whistled straight into my hands.

"So, how about a post pattern?" said Kenny when I got back to him. "I heard you and Uncle David used to run them a lot."

"Yeah, we did. Let's line up at mid-field, okay?"

"You got it," said Kenny, smiling.

I took off down the field and made my cut. I remembered the feeling of waiting for David to throw until it seemed impossibly late, but Kenny waited longer. Then I saw that easy motion, and the ball came at me like a torpedo. It had less arc on it than David's throws ever had, and I could hear it humming as it got closer. Once again I never broke stride, and it sailed into my hands with a velocity that still made them sting, even after travelling fifty-five yards.

As I jogged back the other guys stared at me in stunned amazement. Kenny was still grinning. No wonder, I thought to myself, that things had gotten awkward between the two families. I actually found myself feeling the worst for the two boys. It was impossible for them not to know what the situation was.

"That was cool," he said. "Thanks, man."

"That was more fun than I've had in a long time," I said, panting. "Thanks to you, too."

"Hey, I'm gonna run a few cool-down laps. Are you gonna hang for a while?"

"Sure," I said.

The other kids begged off, and I sat on the field by myself, watching Kenny sail around the track. I told myself I shouldn't have been surprised. His father had always had a terrific arm, too. We'd actually tried out some option plays where Kenny had a chance either to run or throw, but he'd never had any control over his throws, and, besides, all he'd ever wanted to do was put his head down and run over people. When you're a hammer everything looks like a nail, and to Kenny everything looked like a running play. He couldn't convince himself to let go of the ball once he had it in his hands.

The grass beneath me felt good, and running those routes with Kenny Junior had brought back a lot of wonderful memories. But I also had to admit to myself, finally, that it was those memories that had held the seeds of my eventual mediocrity.

I had grown up to cheers: cheers from my teammates; cheers from my schoolmates, and cheers from practically the whole town, week after week. Those cheers every time I caught a touchdown pass from David had given me a visceral thrill, the kind of thrill that could become addictive. And it did. But then I played my last game, and the cheering stopped. People didn't cheer when I got an "A" in Criminology in college, or turned in a term paper on time. They didn't cheer when, as an NYPD cop, I broke up a fight, or prevented a robbery. And they certainly didn't cheer when I finalized a divorce or bailed a drunk out of jail during my disastrous years as a lawyer. I had wanted those cheers; I had needed those cheers, and when I didn't get them I had just quit on myself.

I once again thought of Henry Hudson, and imagined the cheers he must have heard when the *Halfmoon* set sail from the Netherlands on its voyage of destiny to discover the Northwest Passage, only to be followed by his silent, cheerless death in the Canadian wilderness after his mutinous crew had cast him adrift in punishment for his failure.

At least I had a chance, one final chance, at redemption, and I was determined not to waste it.

I glanced at my watch. Kenny Junior ran a six-minute mile as a cool-down, and he wasn't breathing hard when he jogged back over to where I sat. There wasn't a bead of sweat on him.

"Hey, listen," I said. "I'm going over to McDonald's to grab a burger. Wanna come along?"

"Cool," he said.

It was only a five-minute ride to McDonald's, and we rode in silence.

I ordered a Quarter Pounder with Cheese, a Diet Coke, and a small fries. Kenny ordered two Big Mac meals, biggie-sized, with a large Coke. We sat in comfortable silence while we ate our meals. I stared out the window at the beautiful day.

"You gonna eat those fries?"

I looked over at Kenny and realized that he'd eaten his two entire meals in the time it had taken me to eat half of my Quarter Pounder.

"Go ahead," I said, pushing the fries over to him.

"Thanks, man," he said as he shoved his hand into the bag and pulled out almost the entire bagful.

"So, Kenny," I said, ignoring the rest of my burger, "that's one hell of an arm you have."

"Thanks."

"I mean it, Kenny. People always said your Uncle David had the best arm ever to come out of Orange County, but let me tell you, yours is better."

"It is?" he said.

"A lot better," I said. "Kenny, there are NFL quarterbacks who can't throw a post pattern like that."

"Really?"

"Yeah, really. It's a shame you're not playing anymore."

"Donnie's the quarterback, Mr. Hunter. You know that."

"You didn't want to be a running back like your old man, huh?"

"To tell you the truth, Mr. Hunter, I just wasn't that excited about playing football. I guess if I'd been able to play quarterback I would've stuck with it, but otherwise, I have better things to do."

"Like what?"

"I want to be a doctor, Mr. Hunter, and I love music. I play clarinet in the high school band and orchestra, and I play bass for a local rock band. We play the oldies, you know? And I spend a lot of time studying."

"So you're telling me that football's okay, but there are other things you like more, even if you're really good at football."

"I'm good at other things besides football, Mr. Hunter."

"You're a lucky guy, Kenny. Not many people have choices like that."

"Tell my Dad that."

"You can't blame him for being disappointed, Kenny."

"I know," said Kenny, "but sometimes it's tough, you know? Feeling like I'm letting him down."

"He'll understand. Don't worry."

"I hope so."

"What about your Mom?"

"She's really good about it," said Kenny, his eyes lighting up a little. "She wants me to get away from Devon and make my own life. She says she doesn't want me just being a big picture on the wall of the high school." He looked at me and said, "Sorry."

"That's perfectly all right," I said. "Is that why your Mom doesn't want you dating Laura Chandler?"

He gave me a sharp look, and I thought I might have gone too far.

But then he said, "Maybe."

"She thinks that Laura would hold you back if you got serious?"

"Something like that."

"And that doesn't bother you?"

He gave me another long look, like he was trying to decide just how much he was going to share with the relative stranger sitting across from him.

"Look, Mr. Hunter, my mom cares about me. She cares about me a lot. I feel like I ought to respect her wishes. Laura and I talked about it. We're really good friends, and we decided that's how it's gonna be, at least for a while. She's really unhappy about it, but I convinced her that it was for the best. She understands. Laura's something else, you know?"

"And how does your Dad feel about all this?"

"I don't know. Dad's, you know, Dad."

"What do you mean?"

"I don't know. Dad's a great guy, you know?"

"Yes, I do."

"But, I don't know, he just is who he is. He's always out being, you know, Kenny Cooper. He's a great guy, but he hasn't been around for me like Mom has."

Considering my own track record as a father, I didn't have much to say about that.

"So, now can I ask a question?" said Kenny.

"Fair enough," I said.

"What do you think happened to Uncle David? Laura's really worried, and so is Donnie."

"I wish I knew, Kenny."

"Is that why you're being so, like, nosey? So you can find him?"

"I'm sorry, Kenny. I hope I didn't bug you with all the questions."

"It's okay, Mr. Hunter. If I didn't feel like talking, I wouldn't have. But have you learned anything?"

"Oh, Kenny, I've learned a lot."

"Like what?"

"I've learned that the people here aren't the same people I grew up with. They've changed, just like I have. And I'm going to have to work real hard to find your Uncle David."

"I hope you do," said perhaps the most mature person I'd spoken to since I'd returned to Devon-on-Hudson. "He's a cool guy, you know?"

******

When I got back to the apartment there was a cashier's check sitting on the table for the hundred fifty-thousand that David had borrowed, plus the full amount of interest, even though the loan was being repaid early. Doreen clearly wanted the issue closed for good.

It wasn't mid-afternoon yet, and I was feeling antsy after the events of the morning, so I called Lieutenant Hudson at the Midtown South precinct. He told me he'd be there for a few more hours and that I was welcome to come down and drop off the check. He sounded like he was as anxious to get the whole business done with as I was.

The trip down was a snap, and I was walking into the precinct house in a little over an hour. The same young cop was sitting at the front desk, but this time all she did was look up at me and point with her thumb toward the door.

"You know where to find him," was all she said.

When I got to Hudson's office there was a young detective sitting there, and between the two of them, that didn't leave much room for anyone else. The young cop stood up when he saw me coming, perhaps to offer me the chair, but I motioned to him to sit back down. I couldn't help noticing that he was a little shorter than Hudson, perhaps my height, but just as massively built. Where does the NYPD find these guys, I found myself thinking.

"Hi, Matt," said Hudson, reaching out a hand and shaking mine. "I'd like to introduce you to Detective Eduardo Sanchez."

"How do you do, sir?" said Sanchez, shaking my hand. He had a warm smile and a mild manner, but I knew in an instant that he was a man no one should mess with.

"Actually, we were just talking about you," said Hudson. "Look, let's go into the conference room, it'll be more comfortable in there." He pointed to a room catty-cornered to his office. We all went in there and sat down.

"Eduardo," said Hudson, "why don't you tell Matt about your conversation."

"Sure," he said, turning to me. "I was having lunch downtown with one of my old patrol buddies who works out of the 5th Precinct now. Seems that word got around pretty quick about your meeting with Daria Evanishyn and you and Lieutenant Hudson's subsequent, ah, run-in with her enforcer. You met her, so you can imagine she's a pretty well-known to the cops down there, never mind the FBI."

"Yeah, she's pretty tough to miss," I said with a small laugh that I hoped didn't sound nervous.

"Anyway, it seems this guy, his name in Boiko, by the way, is getting a lot of ribbing from his fellow leg-breakers about the beating he took. And you know, it's not the good-natured kind."

"I didn't think it would be," I said.

"I'm sorry, Matt," said Hudson, "I should have thought before I put the guy down."

"Eh," I said, "it was one of those heat-of-the-moment things. Anyway, he had it coming."

"Yeah, he did," said Hudson, still smiling at the memory. I smiled too.

"Anyway," said Sanchez, "the guy has been talking trash to anyone who'll listen about how he's gonna track you down and spread parts of you all over lower Manhattan. That kind of thing. Word is that Daria warned him off, told him it was just business and all that, but the guy's not hearing it."

"Can't blame the guy," I said. "If he doesn't dish out some kind of payback, he's going to have to find a different line of work."

"More like he's gonna have to find a different hemisphere to live in," said Sanchez.

"And I'm sure he's got it figured that it's a better bet to go after me than after an NYPD detective. He know where I live?"

"My buddy doesn't think so," said Sanchez, "mostly because Daria is the only one who knows, and she's not talking. Her and her Ukrainian buddies don't mind going up against the NYPD, but they only do it when they have to, and this lug Boiko's delicate ego is not exactly high on their list of priorities."

"But the point is," said Hudson, "where there's a will, there's a way. He'll find you if he really wants to."

"Gotcha," I said.

"My guess is," said Hudson, "that he'll try to come after you as far away from the city as possible to avoid too much blowback from Daria. So if you're planning any road trips in the near future, you should watch your back. You still have a carry permit?"

"Yeah."

"Good," said Hudson.

I gave Hudson the check. He let out a low whistle when he glanced at the amount, then folded it and put it in his jacket pocket. He looked at his watch and said that he'd get it over to Peter Kwan by the end of the day. He said he'd bring it to Daria Evanishyn personally just for the fun of it, but he didn't want to inflame the situation with Boiko any more than necessary.

I thanked both of them again and left.

There's an awfully good little deli around the corner from the precinct house, and I thought about stopping in and getting a sandwich. It would be a nice break from my steady diet of pizza and Mickey D's. But then I thought that if I wanted a sandwich that bad I could always pick one up at a little place in Devon that I'd recently found called Sally's when I got home.

Home. The word sounded nice to me. I enjoyed the familiar sights and sounds of midtown as I made the short walk up Ninth Avenue to where I'd parked my car, but I really didn't miss the city anymore. I knew where my home was.

CHAPTER TWENTY-SEVEN

'D CALLED DOREEN EARLY the next morning, hoping that I could see her before whatever had gone on the day before with Marianne's visit started to fester. I was relieved when she'd sounded friendly, even happy to hear from me on the phone, and she said she'd have breakfast waiting when I got there.

I almost felt guilty driving past McDonald's. I'd picked up a ham salad and provolone sandwich and some coleslaw from Sally's when I'd gotten back into town the night before, and now I was spurning Mickey for breakfast as well. I found myself secretly hoping that none of the employees would see me when I drove past.

It was the first of July, and even though it was only 7:30 it was already warm outside. But the house had central air, and the kitchen was cool and pleasant as I sat at the table that occupied the center of the room, watching Doreen cook. I'd never seen her cook before. I don't know why, but I was surprised at her quick, practiced movements as she went about her work. She may have had a big house and a lot of money, but she apparently prepared the family meals herself. She was wearing a loose pair of linen slacks and a sleeveless cotton summer blouse. She hadn't put any makeup on yet, and she looked just like she did when we were teenagers. She looked good.

She'd had a pot of coffee on when I got there, and I was on my second cup. The coffee at Doreen's house always tasted better. I told her that I'd delivered the check to Lieutenant Hudson the day before, and she sounded relieved. I didn't bother to tell her about my new friend Boiko. She had enough to worry about, and Boiko wouldn't come after her in any event.

Taking out his revenge against a woman would just make things worse for him.

"Whatever you're cooking, it smells good," I said, hoping that my appetite for breakfast might overcome my appetite for her. It didn't, but I savored the aromas anyway.

"I'm making Eggs Benedict," she said. She turned and looked at me with one of those smiles. "You didn't think I knew how to cook, did you?"

"I guess I never thought about it."

"You thought I went straight from being a Prom Queen to being a Suburban Goddess, complete with a cook and a maid, right?"

"I don't know what I thought."

"I guess you didn't."

"Look, Doreen, I'm really sorry. I guess I'm pretty dense when it comes to understanding women. I certainly didn't understand my own wife." I'd given her an opening to talk about yesterday if she wanted, but she didn't take it.

"You're not supposed to understand, Matt. Don't worry about it."

"I'm beginning to think it's best that way," I said.

She just smiled at me as she brought two plates over to the table and set them down.

The Eggs Benedict were outstanding. The eggs were perfectly poached: the whites firm, and the yolks creamy and rich. The Hollandaise sauce, buttery with that perfect hint of lemon, mixed with the yolks and mated perfectly with the salty Canadian bacon. Whoever Benedict was, he was either a terrific chef or one lucky guy.

"I guess you liked it," said Doreen, as she watched me polish off the eggs. "Do you want me to make you some more?"

"I'd better not," I said. "I'm ten pounds overweight as it is. I can't have you making me fat, now, can I?"

"We'll just have to make sure you get enough exercise," she said as she got up and started clearing the dishes, giving me a look that made me forget about breakfast.

"Can I help with the dishes?" I said.

Doreen laughed out loud.

"Oh, Matt, that's sweet," she said when she stopped laughing, "but this'll only take me a few minutes, and you don't know where anything goes anyway. Just keep me company, okay?"

That was fine with me. There hadn't been much domesticity between Marianne and me for years, and I loved the comfort I felt sitting there in Doreen's kitchen. I also loved watching her body move in all the right ways while she washed and dried.

"Where are the kids?" I said.

"Oh, Donnie's at a summer football practice, and Laura is having a coaching session with her tennis instructor. They'll be out for hours." She turned and looked at me. She couldn't help noticing where my eyes were roaming, and she gave me a quick smile. "Why do you ask?"

"Just wondering."

"Oh," she said, turning back to the sink, her smile turning inward.

"How are they doing, anyway?" I said, trying to get the conversation back on track. "I saw Kenny Junior yesterday and he said they were both pretty upset."

"Kenny Junior spoke to Laura?"

"I don't know. He just said they were upset. He didn't say if he'd been talking to Laura or Donnie."

"Oh."

"Would it bother you if he had been talking to Laura?"

"It would only bother me because I know it bothers Allie, that's all," said Doreen, still facing away from me.

"So, anyway, how are they doing?"

She turned to me but didn't really look at me. "They're a wreck, Matt. They're scared to death. And now it's getting around."

"Are their friends bugging them about it?"

"Nobody's saying anything, but you know how that is."

"Yeah, I do," I said. "And how about you? Are people starting to ask you questions?"

"Not really. I've had a couple of the usual, "Just called to see how things were going" calls, but it's mostly the silent treatment. Frankly, I'd prefer it if they just came out and asked me."

"You holding up okay?"

"I'm getting pretty frantic, too," she said. "I'm not going to lie to you."

She shifted her gaze to me and looked at me for a long time.

"I'm sorry, Matt," she finally said. She put the towel down, returned to the table, and sat down.

"What are you apologizing for? None of this is your fault."

There was another long pause before she finally said, "I'm not just talking about finding David, Matt. I'm not just talking about your investigation. Or maybe I am, I don't know. But I'm talking about you and me, too. I've been sending you all kinds of confusing signals, and it hasn't been fair. Just so you know, they've been just as confusing to me as they must be to you. Sometimes I feel like I'm standing outside myself and watching what I'm doing and just not believing it. So I think it's time to clear the air, not just for the sake of finding David, but for the sake of us, too."

She took me by the hand and stood up.

CHAPTER TWENTY-EIGHT

"**U**S."

The word buzzed in my head like a wasp as she led me into the living room and over to a sofa. She sat down, pulled me down right next to her, and shifted herself so that she was facing me. She didn't let go of my hand.

"I haven't been honest with you about David and me, and that hasn't been fair," she said. "I asked you to find him, and I've drawn you back into my life, but I haven't even had the courage to tell you honestly how things were between us. It seems like all I've been doing is holding out on you while I've been expecting you to find my husband at the same time."

The word "husband" jarred me, and Lacey's admonitions started shouting at my conscience, at least what was left of it. But I kept my mouth shut. Maybe I was learning.

"Things haven't been right between David and me for a long time."

"I know that feeling."

"No, Matt, you don't understand. Things haven't been right between David and me for a very, very long time."

"How long are you talking about?"

She sat quietly. I didn't push her. She looked down at her hand holding mine. She finally looked up at me.

"You're one of the few people who knew how it was."

"How what was?"

"You know, for all of us, growing up. The three of you, and me, I guess. We didn't realize it at the time, but just think about the pressure that was on all of us to be exactly what everyone needed us to be."

"Who was putting pressure on us, Doreen?"

"The whole damn town, Matt! I'm not trying to blame anyone, but think about it. Devon-on-Hudson was just a run-down, lower middle-class backwater back then, remember? Then the three of you came along, and suddenly the town had an identity. People suddenly had a reason to be proud to be from Devon-on-Hudson. They had something to talk about at the barber shop on Saturday and when they got to work on Monday morning. It was like a fairy tale. You guys were the handsome princes and I, heaven help me, was the Enchanted Princess."

"And the tale had to be told," I said, "if I'm following."

"Yes, Matt! And it had to be told just the way everyone needed to hear it."

"'All the world's a stage,' right?"

"Right! And we: you, me, David, and Kenny, we were the players."

"And the players had to stick to the script."

"Yes, or else the whole fairy tale would have evaporated and everybody would have woken up in dumpy old Devon-on-Hudson again. And it would have been our fault."

"Doreen," I said, trying to keep the incredulity out of my voice, "are you saying that you and David never really loved each other? That you got married just because people expected you to? That the Prom King had to marry the Prom Queen so that everybody could live happily ever after?"

"What I'm saying, Matt, is that we got married when we were kids, and we had our kids when we were still kids. Nobody does that anymore, but we did. All I can remember is that we were too young to know what we wanted. We just assumed it was what we wanted because that's how the story went."

"So when did it occur to you that something was wrong?"

"It didn't occur to me for a while, I guess. We had the kids right away, and I was up to my neck in bottles and diapers. David was busy settling into his new job, and of course the pressure was relentless on us to get involved in the town's social and civic activities. Then one day I woke up and realized that David and I hadn't made love in three months."

"Did that upset you?"

"I don't know if it upset me as much as it made me wonder, you know? I'd go out with other women my age and they all talked about how their husbands were just wearing them out. They were young men, after all."

"Did you ever discuss your situation with your friends? I thought women talked about everything."

"What women talk about is none of your business, but no, I didn't discuss it."

"Because the narrative had to be that the Quarterback and the Homecoming Queen had the best sex life ever, right? David and you had to be the best lovers because you were the best at everything."

Doreen looked at me with something approaching admiration.

"That's right," she said.

"I don't mean to pry, Doreen, but was it ever like that?"

"You know, it's funny. I never gave it any thought until well after the fact, but no. All the time we were dating, when we came home for holidays during college, even when we were engaged, David never tried to get me to have sex with him. He was always very polite about it."

"But you had the two kids. There must have been some passion at some point."

"We reproduced, Matt. I don't know how else to describe it."

"You don't think he's gay, do you?"

"Absolutely not."

"How do you know?" I said, recalling my conversation with Richie Glazier.

"Because I just know, that's all. I saw how he looked at other women's asses when we were walking down the street, how a woman in a low-cut dress would turn his head. No, David's not gay."

"Do you think he was having affairs?"

"No, Matt. I do not believe he was having affairs."

I'd heard clients perjuring themselves on the witness stand sound more convincing than that, but I didn't push it.

"Are you saying that he just didn't find you attractive? I find that awfully hard to believe, Doreen."

"I know you do, Matt, and that's sweet."

"So you're saying that you haven't had a sex life since you were young."

"Up until a few years ago, we'd have sex maybe every few months. It would usually be after a party when we'd both had a little too much to drink. That was about it. And then it stopped altogether."

"I apologize for asking this, but did *you* ever have any affairs?"

"That's a fair question. The answer is no."

"I'm sorry, Doreen."

"There's nothing for you to be sorry about. But I'll be forty soon, Matt, and I feel like I've been missing out on something really, really good for way, way too long, and I'm not sure how much longer I'm willing to wait. I don't want to be having this same conversation when I'm fifty, you know?" She gave me a long look that I tried not to make too much of, no matter how much I wanted to.

"It seems like you and I have been in the same boat," I said. "The sex between me and Marianne died years ago. You know what finally killed it?"

"What?"

"One night, when we were in the middle of, you know, intercourse, she looked right at me and said, "You're just imagining I'm Doreen, aren't you?""

"Oh my God, Matt," she said, barely suppressing a smile. "What did you do?"

"I'll tell you what I didn't do."

"I don't think you have to tell me that," she said, now openly grinning.

"You know what the worst part was?"

"What?"

"She was right."

Doreen blushed, and said, "You know, Matt, one of the best things that happened to me in a long time was seeing the look on your face when I first came to visit you at your apartment a couple of weeks ago."

"What do you mean?"

"Knowing that nothing had changed. Knowing that after all these years you still thought I was hot, that you still wanted me. I guess until that moment I didn't realize how much I missed that feeling."

"I thought I was a little more subtle than that."

"Oh, please."

She leaned closer to me and I leaned closer to her. The air seemed to get warmer, while the air conditioning hummed away. I put my hand on her bare arm and pulled her to me...

Somewhere in the kitchen my phone rang. I'd put it on the kitchen counter when I'd arrived, and I'd forgotten all about it.

"I'd better get that," I said, jumping up to run to the kitchen before I had a chance to think twice.

The phone conversation was brief. I also received a text message while I was on the phone. After I'd hung up and read the message I put the phone back on the counter and walked back to the living room.

Doreen was naked when I got back.

"I got tired of waiting for you to take a hint," she said, smiling.

She was still sitting on the sofa, her clothes carefully folded beside her. She stood and walked toward me. Her generous breasts were still firm. Her nipples were dusty pink roses against a blanket of snow. Her stomach was toned and flat. When she got to me she put her hands on my face and kissed me like she meant it, then she reached down and put her hands on my butt and pulled me close.

"I really want to hear about the phone call," she said, her eyes boring into mine. "I just don't want to hear about it right now." She led me back to the sofa.

It had been way too long for both of us, and everything happened pretty fast the first time. The second time took a lot longer, and by the time we were done we were both damp with sweat and breathing like young ponies back from a canter. I think I had a stupid grin on my face. We lay together, not speaking, for a long time.

"You can tell me about the phone call now," she finally said.

"I don't want to," I said.

There must have been something in the tone of my voice, because she looked up at me, her expression suddenly serious.

"Matt?"

"What?"

"Tell me, please."

"The phone call was from Lacey."

She was quiet for a long time. "What did she say?" she finally said.

"She told me that Brad from the bank had called her. David's laptop popped up on the bank's network, and its GPS locator was on."

"Did she tell you where he was?"

"No. I told her we were here, and she said she'd be coming over to talk to us."

"Did she say when?"

"In about an hour," I said, glancing up at a clock on the wall that, almost unbelievably, read just 9 o'clock. It's amazing how little time it takes for a life to change.

"An hour from now?" said Doreen, glancing up at the same clock.

"Yes, and hour from now."

She stood up and gathered up her clothes in one arm. She reached the other hand out to me. "Come with me," she said.

She led me out of the living room and upstairs to her bedroom. She dropped the clothes on the floor and pulled me onto the bed with her.

"I just want to make sure we know where we stand," she said, wrapping her long legs around my torso. I wanted to reply, but my mouth was full of her left breast, and all that came out was a muffled groan. She laughed.

We knew where we stood.

CHAPTER TWENTY-NINE

"**W**ELL, HELLO, YOUNG LOVERS," said my sister as she walked into the kitchen. As usual, she'd let herself in without knocking. Doreen howled.

"What are you talking about?" I said, feeling my face start to burn.

"Oh, for God's sake, Matt. If I had a heat map of this room right now, it would be blinking red where the two of you are standing. Not that I disapprove. I guess I was wrong huh?"

"I guess you were," I said.

"It was a good thing to be wrong about," she said.

"Sure was," I said.

"What are you guys talking about?" said Doreen.

"Nothing important," I said.

Doreen poured coffee for all of us and put on a fresh pot.

"Is that Hollandaise sauce I smell?" said Lacey.

"Yes it is. Matt and I had Eggs Benedict for breakfast. You want me to cook some up for you? It'll only take me a few minutes to whip up some more Hollandaise sauce."

"Sure."

"Haven't you had breakfast yet?" I said.

"Of course I have. What does that have to do with anything? Who in their right mind is going to turn down Eggs Benedict, especially when there's someone in the kitchen who knows how to make a Hollandaise sauce?"

Doreen went to work at the stove while Lacey and I sat at the table and drank coffee, talking about nothing in particular. We didn't want to talk about anything concerning David until Doreen could come and sit down with us. Doreen was just as efficient with the Eggs Benedict as she had been the first time, and she put down a fragrant plate in front of Lacey in what seemed no time. The aroma made me hungry again.

"So, Lace," I said, as Doreen and I watched in wonder while she demolished her meal, "why don't you tell us what's going on?"

"Well, like I told you," she said, pushing her plate away. It looked like it had been licked clean. "Brad had been scanning for David's laptop periodically since we visited the bank. Up until yesterday there was nothing."

"Which meant he had it turned off all this time?" I said.

"Either that, or he'd disabled the GPS tracking," said Lacey.

"I'm guessing he just turned the laptop off," said Doreen. "I'm not sure he'd know how to get into the 'Settings' function to disable the GPS."

"That's my guess, too," said Lacey.

"I wonder why he suddenly turned it on?" said Doreen.

"Perhaps he was trying to contact someone," I said. "Remember, for all he knows, he still owes that money to the Ukrainians. Maybe he was starting to panic."

"Or perhaps he was hoping someone would find him," said Doreen.

"I guess it could be either," I said. "But let's get to first things first. Where is he?"

"He's in a little town called Halfmoon, New York. It's just north of Albany, right where the Mohawk River and the Hudson River meet."

"Huh," I said. "That's an interesting name for a town. Have you ever been there, Doreen?"

"I never heard of the place."

"And David's never mentioned it? Did he perhaps have bank business up there?"

"I never heard him mention it, and I'm just about positive that he never had any bank business up there."

"So am I," I said. "Does Brad think he's still there?"

"He really can't be sure," said Lacey, "but he was there at least until a couple of hours ago."

I stood up.

"Where are you going?" said Doreen.

"I'm going to Halfmoon," I said. "Where else?"

"Now?" said Doreen.

"I'm not sure I have a minute to lose," I said. I gave her a quick kiss and walked out the door.

CHAPTER THIRTY

THE TEXT MESSAGE I'D RECEIVED had been from Eddie Shepherd, telling me that he'd gotten a response on the APB from the Halfmoon police. I called him on the way up and thanked him for the heads up. I didn't tell him about Lacey's phone call. I thought it was best he didn't know about her snooping, and I also didn't want to diminish the fact that he'd reached out to help me.

I had decided to leave directly from Doreen's house, hoping to find David before the trail went cold. It's an easy trip up the Thruway, and I got there in less than two hours. The Hudson River Valley is one of the most scenic areas of the country, and I would have taken the Taconic Parkway to enjoy it if I hadn't been in such a hurry. It was a nice drive anyway.

Halfmoon is, indeed, an interesting name for a town. Some people say it comes from the fact that the bend in the Mohawk River where it flows into the Hudson is shaped life a half moon. But I also knew that it was the name of the ship Henry Hudson sailed when he explored the river that bears his name on his search for the Northwest Passage. I guessed that it was probably somewhere near this spot that Henry decided he wasn't going to be finding it anytime soon, that perhaps God had played a trick on him. The facts were probably on the side of the first explanation, but I had a soft spot for the latter.

Route 9 runs through Halfmoon, but it's not a busy place. There's a McDonald's, a Subway, a couple of drugstores, and a dry cleaner; but the residents have to travel a few miles up Route 9 toward Saratoga to do any major shopping. I drove by a place called the Halfmoon Diner, which looked inviting. There's also a Best Western. It wasn't the only motel in town, but it would be the first one someone would notice driving in from the highway. David's laptop had once again gone silent, but I figured the most likely places to stake out would be either the diner or the motel. It was past noon, and I was hungry. I rationalized that at that hour David would be more likely to be out looking for a meal than hanging out in a motel room. I pulled into the parking lot of the diner.

The Halfmoon Diner didn't look like much from the road, but the interior was surprisingly spacious. They could certainly serve a lot of people in the place, and from the look of the lunchtime crowd there, I bet they did. I took a seat in a back corner that gave me a pretty good view of the rest of the dining area and perused the menu, which was expansive, to say the least. It turned out that the Halfmoon was a typical Greek diner: You could get breakfast all day, plus it offered a full lunch and dinner menu, and they had a liquor license. Chances were if you were hungry for something, it would be on the menu. I was starting to like the place already.

A waitress came by with coffee and a glass of ice water. I decided that I should have a substantial meal, since I didn't know when I'd have the chance to eat again, so I ordered the broiled calf's liver and onions and mashed potatoes. One of the most tragic consequences of modern dietary dogma is that organ meat has been deemed unhealthy, and it's more and more difficult to find restaurants that serve it. I bitterly opposed that notion, and I ordered liver, sweetbreads, and scrapple whenever I had the chance, especially since Marianne wouldn't even hear of serving them at home. I made a mental note to ask Doreen where she stood on the issue.

In just a few minutes the waitress came by and set my meal in front of me. She smiled at me. I took that as a vote of approval for the liver and onions.

The liver was everything I hoped it would be: hot, tender, perfectly cooked, and bathed in a rich, brown gravy. The onions were tender and sweet, and the mashed potatoes were smooth and buttery. A side of peas was served on a separate plate, and I immediately deposited them on top of my potatoes. Peas are, of course, the only acceptable side vegetable for liver and onions. I dug in hungrily, and I had almost forgotten why I was there when David Chandler walked in the front door.

******

I wanted to jump up and greet him, but I held back. Perhaps it was because I'd just climbed out of bed with his wife only a few hours ago, but I didn't think so. I felt strangely not guilty about that. I think it was more because of David. He took a table at the other end of the diner from where I was sitting and said a few words to the waitress. He was probably only ordering coffee, but the way they were talking made me feel like they knew each other. He didn't look around the restaurant. Instead, he stared out the window, like he was waiting for somebody. My observation was bolstered by the fact that the waitress had set the table for two.

I looked at my old friend as I worked my way through my meal. He really hadn't changed. His light hair was still thick and showed no hint of graying, and his handsome features were still sharp. He was tall and well built, probably no more than ten pounds over his playing weight. He moved with the easy confidence of an athlete. He was the type of guy who people noticed when he walked into a room, just like the way people had noticed him all those years ago when he'd jogged onto the football field. Even after all I'd learned during my search for him, I still found it hard to believe that the man was a failure.

The waitress brought his coffee to him, but he waved her off when she appeared to ask him if he wanted to order yet. She nodded and left.

I was almost finished with my meal, and I badly wanted a piece of the cherry pie I'd spied in the pastry counter on the way in. But I didn't want to call attention to myself, so I slowly savored the rest of my liver. It wasn't difficult.

Just as I was finishing my last bite David seemed to react to something he saw out the window. He stood up suddenly and walked toward the entrance of the diner.

A woman walked in, and David's face lit up as he went to her and gave her a hug and a long, lingering kiss. He and Doreen may have suffered through a passionless marriage, but even from this distance there was no mistaking the passion in that kiss. They walked back to David's booth arm in arm, and the woman sat down opposite him. They reached across the table and clung to each other's hands. David's face was alive as he talked to the woman.

It was clear to anyone who cared to notice that David Chandler was in love with Allison Sawyer Cooper, and that she was in love with him.

I left enough cash on the table to pay for the liver and onions plus a generous tip for the nice waitress and slipped out the side door, although I could have marched right by the two of them singing "The Star Spangled Banner" and I don't think they would have noticed me.

I swung by the McDonald's and got myself a cup of coffee, then drove over to the Best Western and parked in a spot between two other cars. I cracked the window open halfway and settled in. The outside air was cool and dry, and I wouldn't be uncomfortable. The coffee would give me trouble sooner rather than later, but I wasn't worried. I didn't think I was going to have to wait long.

I was right. In less than an hour two cars pulled into the parking lot, and David and Allie walked hand in hand into the motel.

I rolled up my car window and pulled out of the parking lot. I would learn nothing by storming into their hotel room; I knew exactly what I would find.

I had done my job, and I had done it well: I had found David Chandler. Nobody cheered, but it felt awfully good.

CHAPTER THIRTY-ONE

"**W**HY'D YOU BRING SO MANY DONUTS?" I said to the woman I loved.

We were sitting at the tiny table in the tiny kitchen of the sterile duplex that I knew would never be my home. I'd wanted to see Doreen as soon as I'd gotten back the night before, but her kids had been home, and she hadn't wanted to leave them alone. Under the circumstances I couldn't blame her. I'd told her what I thought she needed to know over the phone, but all she'd said was, "Look, now's not the time." I guess I hadn't known what to expect, but I hadn't expected that. She'd agreed to stop by my place in the morning. I hadn't slept well.

She'd brought coffee and a dozen donuts from Dunkin' Donuts with her. We both drank some coffee and I was munching on a donut, but Doreen ignored them.

"I figured Lacey would get here sooner or later," she said, tiredly. "You know your sister; she's too curious to stay away." It was clear that she hadn't slept well either, and for the first time since I'd come back, Doreen almost looked her age. But she wasn't exactly acting heartbroken, or even all that upset.

"Doreen," I said, putting down my coffee cup, "I don't know where you want me to go from here. I guess I don't even know how you're feeling about all this."

"I don't either," she said. She stood up and put the box of donuts and the empty coffee cups on the counter. It was a hot day, and she was wearing denim shorts and a tee shirt. Despite the fatigue, the heat, and the stress of the moment, I felt a pang of desire.

"I feel like there's still so much we don't know," I said, dutifully redirecting my attention.

"But what's the point?" said Doreen. "What will it possibly change?"

"You've been married to the guy for almost twenty years. Don't you want to know?"

"I'm trying to decide."

"I'm just trying to understand how you're feeling," I said. "Are you sad, angry, surprised?"

"I guess all of that and none of it," she said. "How did you feel the day you finally knew your marriage was over?"

"It'd been coming for so long, I guess I'm not even sure I knew when that day was. So I guess I didn't feel much of anything."

"That's kind of how I feel."

"But, Doreen, there's been a betrayal here. That has to hurt."

"It's not like I didn't somehow know something was terribly wrong. And, besides, I've engaged in my own betrayal, haven't I."

"So have I, I guess."

"So maybe it's a matter of we're all finally getting what we wanted all along."

"Except Kenny."

"Yes, Kenny," said Doreen.

"Do you have any idea how long this has been going on?"

"None. It could've been going on for years for all I know, or it could be like what happened to you and me."

"What do you mean?"

"You know," she said. "You live a certain way for a long time for any number of reasons, probably mostly inertia. Then one day something happens, maybe something small, but it makes you realize that you can't live like that another day. All it took for me was for you to show up. I hadn't even seen you yet, but when I heard you were back in town it was like something woke up inside me. I knew I was at the end of the life I'd been living. Maybe it was the same for Allie and David."

"Or maybe not."

"Or maybe not. I'm not sure I need to know," she said, staring out the kitchen window.

"But where does the money fit into all of this?" I said. For some reason I stared out the window, too.

"I wish I could tell you. It just makes no sense. I know he's given Allie a lot of money over the years, but I'm pretty sure she had to spend at least most of it. And what are they going to do with $150,000? Sure, it's a lot of money, but it's not like David could quit his job and they could run away together and live happily ever after on it."

"They could last on it long enough to get back on their feet somewhere else."

"Maybe," said Doreen, "but I just can't make myself believe that's what it was for. He knew he was going to have to pay it back. Even if he didn't understand the full implications of the interest, he had to have understood the risks of borrowing from people like that, so it makes absolutely no sense that he'd literally risk his life for it just to leave me after all these years. I'm sorry, that is absolutely crazy."

"So if it wasn't that, what? What could have made him so desperate for that money?"

"I've been giving that a lot of thought, Matt, but I just can't come up with anything that would drive David to do something that risky rather than just be honest with me. And no matter what condition our marriage was in, David was a devoted father. His life revolved around his kids. What would make him desert them? Remember, I'm not the only one who stuck with an unhappy marriage. So did he. There was nothing more important in his life than those kids, especially not his own personal happiness."

"I love my kids, too, Doreen. But I finally had to leave."

"Not to put too fine a point on it, Matt, but I'm not Marianne. If she hadn't driven you out of that marriage, do you honestly think you would have been the one to ask for the divorce?"

"Absolutely not."

"Because of the kids, right?"

"Yes. Right."

"I've been as good a wife as I could be, Matt. I've been a good mother, and despite everything, David has been a devoted father. I never gave him any reason to leave me, and I never gave him any reason to think that I wanted to leave him. And David, to his credit, has been the same. He has never done anything to hurt me, embarrass me, or give me any reason to think that he wanted to leave me. His reputation is spotless in this community, and that means almost as much to him as his kids do."

I reached over and grabbed the box of donuts off the counter and grabbed a jelly donut.

"Sorry," I said. "All this thinking is making me hungry."

"Me, too," said Doreen, pulling out a Chocolate Glazed.

The front door opened and slammed shut, making us both jump.

"I smell donuts," my sister called out.

"Come on in," I called back, "as if you needed asking."

"Hi guys," said Lacey as she walked into the kitchen, picked up the donut box and peered in. "What, no Bavarian Cream?"

"Don't look at me," I said. "Doreen picked them out."

"So, you don't want any nookie today, huh, bro?" said Lacey as reached pulled out a Chocolate Filled.

Doreen cracked up, and so did I.

"So, how goes the investigation, Mr. Marlowe," said Lacey after the laughter died down.

I told her about my trip to Halfmoon, and Doreen recounted the discussion we'd just been having in detail. We were beyond keeping our personal lives private; we just wanted to solve the mystery of David's behavior.

"Huh," said Lacey, pulling out a Honey Glazed. She took a bite.

"'Huh,' what?" I said.

"It sounds to me like you've got your answer."

"What?!" Doreen and I both said at the same time.

"It's pretty obvious to me."

"What's so obvious?" I said.

"No, Matt," she said, swallowing the last bite of her donut. "I told you a long time ago that if you started digging into this you were going to find out a lot of things that you didn't want to know."

"I already have," I said.

"You're not finished," said Lacey, fishing through the donut box. "You're not even close."

"What's that supposed to mean?"

"You're going to have to find that out for yourself. I'm not going to help you on this one."

"Maybe we're better off not knowing," said Doreen.

"No, Doreen, you're not," said Lacey, looking more serious than I'd ever seen her look. "It's too late now. You have to find out." She grabbed another donut, a powdered jelly, and headed for the door.

"Where are you going?" I called out after her.

"Where do you think I'm going? I'm going to get some coffee. Donuts make me thirsty."

The door banged shut behind her.

******

"What else am I supposed to do?" I said to Doreen as we sat at my kitchen table, staring at the empty donut box.

"I don't know, Matt," said Doreen, "but I just don't know what going back to Halfmoon and confronting him is going to accomplish."

"I think it'll make him do something, one way or the other. If he still thinks the Ukrainians are going to come after him for that money, he'll hide forever. And frankly, I don't want this kind of a stalemate. I want to move ahead with my own life, Doreen. I'm in love with the man's wife, in case you haven't noticed, and sooner or later I'm going to have to look him in the eye and tell him that."

"I love you, too, Matt," said Doreen, but she looked frightened when she said it.

"You're not having second thoughts, are you?"

"No, I'm not. But do you have any idea what's going to happen in this town when all this comes out? I'm worried about the kids."

"I am, too. But we didn't start this."

"And David's not going to volunteer to finish it, is he."

"It sure doesn't look like it," I said.

"And the longer we wait, the worse it will be for the kids."

"Yes, Doreen. That's right."

"And the longer we wait, the worse we're going to look in the kids' eyes."

"I'm afraid so."

"And we're never going to figure out what Lacey was talking about just sitting here, are we?"

"No, we're not," I said. "I don't understand why she just won't come out and tell us. This isn't some game we're playing here."

"I think your sister learned a long time ago," said Doreen after a long hesitation, "that there are some things you have to figure out for yourself. That's how she saved herself. It didn't matter how many people told her what she was doing to herself; it was the figuring it out herself part that was important. She knows that this is not a game, Matt. Not for David, not for Allie and Kenny, and certainly not for you and me."

"I guess you're both right, but for the life of me I can't figure out what she's talking about."

"I can't either," said Doreen. "I keep going over our conversation, but I just don't see it. Which is all the more reason to confront David, I guess."

"I think so, too. I don't think we have a choice."

"Do you want me to come with you?"

"Thanks, but not this time."

"No cheerleaders allowed in the huddle, right?" said Doreen.

That shut me up. I hadn't thought about it like that, but it was true. No cheerleaders allowed in the huddle. This had to be between David and me, one last time. Doreen stood up, put the empty donut box back on the counter, and headed out of the kitchen.

"Where are you going?" I said.

"I'm going home and going for a swim," said the love of my life.

It sounded nice, but I had to huddle up first.

CHAPTER THIRTY-TWO

I COULD HAVE LOITERED IN THE PARKING LOT of the Best Western, but I thought it would be a waste of time. I'd swung by Kenny and Allie's house on the way out of town, and Allie's car had been in the driveway. And I didn't think David would hang around in his room and watch TV. Besides, the Halfmoon Diner had impressed me as kind of an addictive place, and I bet he'd be back there again for lunch.

The waitress remembered me and seated me at the same booth I'd had the day before. She must have been impressed by the tip. I ordered coffee and told her I was waiting for someone before I ordered. She nodded and went off to get my coffee.

It didn't take long. The waitress was just setting my coffee cup on the table when David walked in and sat down at the same booth he'd occupied the day before. But today was different. He didn't look fidgety, and he wasn't staring out the window. When the waitress stopped at his table he picked up his menu and ordered his lunch. She didn't put down a second place setting. There was no sense in putting this off any longer. I picked up my coffee cup and walked over to my old friend.

"Hello, David."

His first expression was one of sheer panic. I wasn't surprised, because I was positive that Allie would have told him about me, that I was looking for him, and that I knew about the money. But, as all good quarterbacks do, he recovered quickly.

"Matt, my God! What a pleasant surprise! Please, sit down," he said, greeting me like I was a prospective customer at the bank. He didn't offer to shake my hand, which was fine with me.

"It can't be that much of a surprise, David," I said, taking my seat and putting my coffee cup on the table. The waitress came by and I ordered a tuna sandwich. She seemed a little crestfallen, but this was not going to be a liver and onions kind of a discussion, and I didn't want a delicacy going to waste

"What do you mean?" said David, trying to look innocent.

"David, you've been missing for over two weeks. Doreen and the kids are frantic."

"Look, Matt. It's okay. I just had a few things to work out, and I didn't want to burden Doreen, that's all. Please tell her that I'll be back in a few days and I'll explain everything. Everything will be okay."

"David, we know about the $150,000, and we know where you got it."

He paled at that. Allie had told him I knew about the money, but she didn't know where it had come from, so how did I?

"I can explain all that," he finally said after a long pause.

"It's all been repaid, just so you know. Doreen paid it back, including the interest. Jesus, David. What were you thinking?"

The relief on David's face was palpable. I'd been right: He'd just run because he was scared; it was nothing more complicated than that.

"But she told me we didn't have the money! How did she repay it?"

"That's none of your business right now. She just did, and you're off the hook."

"That's good, Matt. That's good. Thanks for telling me."

"So."

"'So' what?"

"What was the money all about?"

"Look, I tried to explain this all to Doreen, but she didn't listen to me. If she had, all this never would have happened."

"So why don't you explain it all to me."

"Allie needed the money, Matt," said David, fidgeting. "She needed it badly. Kenny's always had a problem with his gambling, and it all of a sudden got a lot worse. He made a really big bet with some really bad people, and he lost. He's my friend, Matt; he's *our* friend. I had to help him."

"Bullshit," I said, perhaps a little too loudly, just as the waitress came by with our food. David had ordered an omelet, and it smelled great. I looked down at my tuna sandwich and wondered if I'd made the wrong choice. The waitress gave me a dirty look and left.

"What do you mean, Matt? And watch your language, okay? This is a family establishment."

"Okay, then. Baloney. Kenny doesn't have a gambling problem."

"What do you mean? Are you saying Allie's been lying to me all this time?"

"I don't think Allie was the one doing the lying, David. And, by the way, nice job of throwing your girlfriend under the bus."

"Girlfriend?" said David, doing a bad job of looking shocked. "What are you talking about?"

"I was here yesterday, too, David."

David reddened. He took a bite of his omelet to buy himself some time. I took the opportunity to take a bite of my sandwich. They made good tuna salad here, and it tasted good in a non-liver-and-onions kind of way.

"I don't know what you thought you saw, Matt," he said, after taking his time swallowing, "but Allie and I are just friends, that's all."

"I saw what I saw, David. And I also followed the two of you back to the hotel."

"Look, Matt," said David, his expression hardening. "This is none of your business. I can explain this all to Doreen, and I will. You were a good friend, but you've been away a long time, and it's time for you to butt out. Doreen and I are very important to our community, and I'm not going let you sully my standing."

I thought the 'my' was interesting, but I decided to ignore it. "It's too late for that, David."

"What do you mean?"

"David, when you get home Doreen is going to ask you for a divorce."

"What?" he said, a note of panic in his voice. "Over this? She can't do that to me!"

"It's not because of the money, and it's not because you disappeared. And it's not because of whatever is going on between you and Allie. It's because of me, David. Doreen and I are in love, and we want to be together."

I didn't know what to expect. Would he reach across the table and punch me? Would he throw his food at me? Would he burst into tears?

"Oh," he said. A calculating look spread over his face, and I could watch him thinking as he hesitated long seconds before replying. "So, you mean, nobody would think the divorce was my fault?" he finally said.

For a few seconds, I was too stunned to reply.

"People will think what they want to think, David," I finally said. "I'm not interested in blaming anyone for anything. I just want Doreen."

"So, what do we tell the kids?"

"That's up to you and Doreen."

"But they won't blame me, right?"

I didn't know what to say. I'd just told my oldest, my best, friend that I was in love with his wife of twenty years, and I'd barely gotten a reaction.

"David, I don't know, I-." I got no further.

David's phone rang. It was one of those cheap flip phones that you buy along with a fixed amount of phone time, and they were impossible to trace. The crooks I used to chase in New York called them "burners." He dropped his fork and answered it like the guy on the other end was going to tell him he'd won the Irish Sweepstakes.

"Hello?" he said, looking serious. He listened intently for a few seconds. Then he looked up at me and said, "Hey, I've got to step away for a minute. I'll be right back. Why don't you order us some dessert?" Then he got up and left the table, heading for the lobby.

The only thing that disappointed me was that he thought he was fooling me. There hadn't been anyone on the other end of the line. While we were talking he'd self-dialed his phone, and it hadn't taken much to see him doing it.

I took a final bite of my sandwich while I watched him sneak out the door and head for his car.

It didn't matter. I'd done what I'd come to do: I'd rousted him out of his perch. I'd found out all that I was going to find out from him sitting here in the Halfmoon Diner, and I knew where he was going. What he did from that point would tell me everything I wanted to know. I waited until I saw his car pull out of the parking lot, then I asked for the check. I left enough cash on the table to settle the bill and leave the waitress another nice tip.

It wasn't until I got up to leave that I saw another car pull into the parking lot.

******

It's not hard to spot trouble coming when it pulls into a diner parking lot in Halfmoon, New York in a black, late-model Dodge Challenger with smoked glass all around.

The car pulled in diagonally across two parking spaces off to the side of the diner, and the driver opened the door and got out. He was holding a baseball bat in his right hand. I guess he figured a .45 slug to the head would be too good for me, or not enough fun for him. He didn't bother to lock the car.

The bullet head was the same, but Boiko wasn't wearing a suit this time, just a cutoff muscle shirt that exposed a six-pack and arms the size of most people's thighs, and a pair of running shorts that exposed thighs the circumference of sewer pipes. His nose looked grotesquely swollen, and I guessed it had been badly broken when Lieutenant Hudson had planted him in the sidewalk. I figured he was too embarrassed to go to a doctor and get it fixed.

I still carried a gun, a Smith & Wesson .38, but I'd left it in the glove compartment of my car, thinking the guy wouldn't come at me in broad daylight in a public place in a quiet town. But of course he would, I now realized: that would be the whole point.

Looking at the guy, I knew that something would have to break my way or I was more than likely a dead man. I'm a big man, an ex-cop, and I'm good in a fight; but compared to him I was small, and the basic rule of fighting is that a good big man will always beat a good small man.

Then something broke my way.

Instead of heading for the front entrance, he headed for the side entrance to the diner that was nearest to his car, but that door is always locked from the outside, and it's heavy. The only other entrance is the back door that leads from the kitchen out to the dumpsters. I knew that's what he'd try next.

I headed over to the swinging doors that led back to the kitchen and walked through. A waitress was coming the other way, and it looked like she was going to say something to me until she saw the look on my face. She just kept on walking.

The kitchen was noisy, chaotic, steamy, and suffocatingly hot. Waitresses were shouting at the cooks, and the cooks were shouting back. Busboys were racing in with buckets piled high with dirty dishes that they deposited with a crash near the commercial dishwasher and raced back out with armloads of clean dishes that they deposited back at the cooks' stations. The stovetops were covered with broiling hot frying pans that even the cooks, with their calloused, scarred hands handled with dry dishtowels.

I grabbed a dry towel from one of the busboys and walked over to the stoves. I grabbed the nearest frying pan, a heavy skillet with a nice-looking steak frying in it. At least it wasn't liver, I thought, as I dumped the meat onto the floor.

"Hey, what the fuck?" said a cook, but I ignored him and headed toward the back door.

I didn't expect the guy to knock, and he didn't disappoint me. The door exploded open as he came charging through the door with his head down. But before he had a chance to get his bat-wielding arm inside the door I let him have it in the face with the cooking side of the frying pan. He screamed as the broiling hot fat from the steak hit his face and the pan smashed what was left of his nose. He started to spin around like a wounded animal, the baseball bat in his hand forgotten. But as much pain as he was in, and even without the bat, I knew the man could still kill me with a swing of one of his fists.

When his back was to me, I swung the stove side of the heavy pan at the back of his head as hard as I could. I felt something give, and I didn't think it was the pan. The guy let out a soft moan and seemed to stagger a step before he collapsed in a heap. I didn't think he'd get up. I hoped I hadn't killed him.

I dropped the pan and walked back through the kitchen. "I think you ought to call 911," I said to the first waitress I saw, then I walked back through the dining room and out the front door. I pulled out of the parking lot slowly, hoping that no one would get my plate number; I knew that someone telling the cops that they saw me drive away in a Honda

Accord would be less than worthless. But I couldn't worry about that right now. What would be would be.

I pulled back on to Route 9 thinking that I would probably never see Halfmoon again, and that I might have missed my last, best chance to try the cherry pie.

CHAPTER THIRTY-THREE

I THOUGHT ABOUT FOOTBALL A LOT on the way back to Devon-on-Hudson, and by the time I pulled into Doreen's driveway I had it figured out.

She was out by the pool, wearing that black one-piece that covered about as little as a one-piece could.

"Matt," she said, getting out of her seat. "I didn't expect you back so soon."

"I'm an ex-cop," I said. "Cops never learn how to drive slow. Doreen, I promise this will be the last time I'll ever say this to you, but please, get dressed."

"What? Why? What are we doing?"

"We're going over to Kenny and Allie's house. I'm willing to bet David's already there, so we have to hurry."

Doreen froze.

"He knows about everything. But what's more important, so do I, and he doesn't know that yet. Please, honey, go get dressed. I don't think they're going to be at the house for too long and I don't want to miss them. It'll be all right, I promise."

"I like that," she said, her frightened expression melting into a smile.

"Like what?" I said.

"You called me 'honey.' It sounded nice."

"It felt nice, too," I said, smiling back. I couldn't help it. "But please, go get changed!"

She ran off. It took everything I had not to follow her. But then I reminded myself that I was about to shatter her world. I sat down and waited.

******

The drive over to Kenny and Allie's house took only five minutes. There wasn't time to explain everything to Doreen, and I didn't try. It was going to be rough for her either way. When we got there David's Audi and Allie's SUV were both in the driveway. I said a silent prayer of thanks that Kenny's Jeep wasn't there.

The front door opened just as I was about to knock, and I saw David, with the same look of terror on his face that I'd seen at the Halfmoon Diner, and Allie looking just as pleased to see me as the first time. Allie was holding an overnight bag in one hand. She paled when she saw Doreen, but she and David both recovered quickly.

"Hi, David. Hi Allie," I said. I think we need to talk, don't you?"

"I can't see where we have anything to discuss," said David, putting on a pretty respectable show of righteous indignation.

"I think you're wrong," I said, opening the door and walking in. Doreen followed me.

"Hello, David," she said, giving her husband a level stare.

"Doreen," said David. "I can't tell you how shocked I was to learn about what's been going on behind my back. I don't know how you're ever going to be able to hold your head up in this town again."

"I think it's going to hold up just fine," said Doreen.

"Okay, David, let's cut the crap," I said.

"I don't know what you're talking about," said David.

"David, like I told you, I saw what I saw. I saw the two of you together yesterday at the Halfmoon Diner. I saw the two of you slipping into the Best Western."

"I don't know what you think you saw," said David, "but I'll tell you exactly what it was. Allie is a dear friend of mine, and she came to see me because she thought I ought to know what was going on between the two of you."

I had to be impressed at the speed with which David was putting his narrative together. If he'd only put that much effort into his job maybe he would have been a better banker.

"Number one, David," I said, "Allie had no way of knowing about Doreen and me. And number two, I don't think I've ever seen 'dear friends' kiss each other the way you two did at the diner."

"That's just your version," said David. "For all anybody knows, you're just making that up to excuse your behavior."

"I'm proud of my behavior, David," I said. "I'm not sure you can say the same. And, by the way, Allie, what do you have in that overnight bag? Milk and cookies for a snack at the lake?"

"That's none of your damn business!" said Allie.

"No, it's not," I said, "and I don't particularly give a warm crap what's in there, but I can guess."

"Now look here, Matt," said David. "I don't think you're in any position to be making any accusations. You admitted to me at the diner that you were carrying on an affair with my wife."

"And now you're seeking solace in the arms of your best friend's wife, is that it? Does Kenny know about this?"

"You leave Kenny out of this!" said Allie.

"Maybe I should," I said. "It's obvious that you are."

"Enough, Matt," said David. "Look, Allie and I have been close friends for many years. It's only natural that I would seek her out once I found out what had been going on."

"And in the course of that heartbreaking discussion you discovered that you might have stronger feelings than friendship for Allie, is that it?"

I could see the wheels spinning in David's head.

"Yes. Yes, that's right," he said after giving it a few moments consideration. "I opened up to her, and that enabled her to open up to me. I was shocked to learn that she and Kenny had been very unhappy for a long time. Of course, who can be surprised at that? Look at the man, for God's sake. He's a buffoon."

"Nice guy, David," I said. "I thought the man was your best friend."

"That doesn't matter," said David. "What matters is that due to some tragic circumstances completely beyond our control, most importantly Doreen's betrayal of me and Kenny's failure as a husband and provider,

Allie and I are discovering that we have feelings for each other. No one would ever criticize us for that."

"Except that's not the truth, is it?" I said.

"What are you talking about?" said David.

"Look," I said, "we have a lot more to talk about, and both of you know it, so why don't we sit down in the living room and talk this out?"

"David," said Allie, "I want to leave now. This is all very upsetting."

"It's about to get a lot more upsetting," I said, heading toward the living room, giving David and Allie no choice but to follow.

Once we were seated I turned to Doreen. "Doreen, I'm sorry that this is all coming out like this. But there was just no time."

"Matt, it's not your fault," she said. "I've been avoiding the truth my entire life. If this is the day I finally have to face it, so be it."

I was proud of her, but that wasn't going to make this any easier.

"You know, David," I said, "I spent the drive back down here thinking."

"Bravo for you," said my old friend.

"I've been thinking about football."

"Oh, for God's sake, Matt," said Allie, "that's all ancient history. What does it have to do with anything?"

"But it does, doesn't it?" I said, turning to Allie.

"Matt, could you please get to whatever point you're trying to make?" said David.

"I was thinking in particular," I said, keeping my eyes on Allie, "of that game against Cornwall in our junior year."

"Yeah, so?" said Allie, but something feral, something like basic dread, was creeping into her eyes.

"It's the story we all talked about a thousand times, right? About how you and Kenny had that Romeo and Juliet moment while we were out on the field for the coin toss. I don't think we all ever got together without repeating that story."

"Matt," said David, "what are you getting at?"

"It's a funny thing about stories," I said. "The more you repeat them the more you believe that the version you're telling is what really happened. We're all human, and we all do it."

"Matt," said Doreen, "you're even starting to confuse me."

"See that?" said David, starting to stand, "Even your girlfriend here thinks you're full of crap."

"Sit down, David," I said, keeping my eyes on Allie. It must have been my old cop's voice, because David sat right back down. "But that's not what really happened, is it, Allie?"

"I don't know what you're talking about," she said.

"Sure you do," I said. "I guess it was seeing the two of you hugging and kissing at the diner that finally woke me up, that made me recall that moment the way it really was."

"Oh, come on, Matt," said David.

"You weren't looking across the field at Kenny, were you, Allie?"

"Jesus," said Doreen.

"David, make him stop," said Allie.

"You were staring at David. David was the one you wanted all along, but you couldn't have him. So you took what you could get, right? At least that way you had a built in excuse to be around David all the time."

"Well," said Allie, "if Miss Prom Queen here hadn't been standing in the way, maybe none of this ever would have happened."

"Dammit, Allie!" said David, "What the hell are you saying?"

"I'm sorry, David," she said, reddening.

"It's okay," said David. "It's just the four of us. Just don't say it again, okay?"

"Okay," said Allie, but she was rattled, and I knew it would get easier from there.

"And remember that rumor about the abortion our senior year?" I said. I was only guessing, but I knew I was right.

"Matt, don't," said Allie.

"We always believed it was a lie because Kenny swore that you two had never had sex. And he was telling the truth, wasn't he?"

"Yes, he was," said Allie.

"But you *did* have that abortion, didn't you?"

"Oh, my God," murmured Doreen.

"Goddammit, Matt, cut it out!" David once again rose from the sofa.

"Sit down, David," I said. "We're not finished here."

"I think we are!"

"Oh, no we're not," I said, glaring at him. "Oh, no we're not, not by a long shot, and you know it, David."

"Matt," said Doreen, "what are you talking about?"

"I don't know," said David, "but I do know that Allie and I shouldn't have to listen to another word of this nonsense."

"Yes, you do," said a voice from the stairway.

We all turned in the direction of the voice.

It was Kenny Cooper, Junior.

******

"KENNETH!" cried his mother. "How long have you been here?"

"I was upstairs in my room when you came in. I started to come down to say 'hi,' but once I heard what you were talking about, I stopped. I didn't know what to do, so I just stood here."

"I'm sorry you had to hear all this, sweetheart," said Allie. "You must be terribly upset. We'll talk it over, I promise."

"It's all right, Mom," said Kenny. "I pretty much knew about everything anyway."

"What?!" said Allie, her face paling as she looked up at her son, who slowly walked down the stairs and into the living room. He made no attempt to sit down.

"Like I said, it's all right, Mom," he said, and then he turned to me. "Mr. Hunter, could you please finish what you were starting to say? I've been waiting for someone to help me with this for a long time."

I stared at him for a long moment.

"How did you know, Kenny?" I said.

"Matt," said Doreen, "what's going on here?"

"I'm really sorry, Doreen," I said, "but you were going to have to find out about this one way or another."

"Remember, Mr. Hunter," said Kenny, "how I told you that I wanted to be a doctor?"

"Yes."

"Well, I took AP Biology last year, a year ahead of most of the other kids. Early in the first semester we did a section on genetics, and we did studies of genotypes and phenotypes, and dominant and recessive genes and all that stuff."

"What are you talking about?" said Allie, but David had turned white.

"So, we did blood typing on ourselves. It turned out I was type AB positive. But I also knew that you have type B blood Mom, and Dad has type O."

"How did you know that?" I asked.

"I asked Dad," said Kenny.

"So he doesn't know," I said.

"Naw. And you know Dad. I knew he'd never want to know why I asked. I just told him I was doing something for school and he told me."

"Doesn't know what?" said Doreen. Allie and David were now both frozen solid.

"You see, Mrs. Chandler," said Kenny, "we all have two genes for blood type. If Mom is type B, she can either have two "B" genes or one "B" gene and one "O" gene. There are no other possibilities. And since the "O" gene is recessive, Dad had to have two "O" genes to have type O blood."

"I'm sorry, Kenny," said Doreen. "I was never any good at this stuff. What are you getting at?"

"Like I said, I'm type AB positive, Mrs. Chandler. One of my parents had to give me an "A" gene, but neither one of my parents could have done that. So one of my parents is not one of my parents."

"And then what did you do?" I said.

"I was with Laura one day and I asked her if she knew what her parents' blood types were. She was taking the same course I was, so I figured she'd know."

"And what did she tell you?" I said.

"She told me that you, Mrs. Chandler, are type O, and you, Mr. Chandler, are type A." I couldn't help noticing that he'd dropped the whole "Uncle David" and "Aunt Doreen" thing.

Doreen looked like she was going to faint, and I put my arm around her. She was shivering.

"Oh, come on, Kenny," said David, sinking lower than I thought was possible, even for him, "there are millions of people with type A blood out there."

"Oh, David," said Allie. The scales were starting to fall from her eyes, but she had too much to lose at this point.

"Are you going to deny that you're my father? Are you, Mr. Chandler?"

"Kenny, it's just that…"

"Look at me, Mr. Chandler. Look at me!"

"I'm not denying anything, Kenneth," said David, without making eye contact. "I've helped support you all these years, for Heaven's sake. The reason I got myself into all this trouble is because I knew your Mom needed money for your college education, and I wasn't going to let either of you down."

"I practically had to beg you, for God's sake," said Allie.

"Allie," said David, "I've already explained this to you…"

"I'm betting that you didn't have to beg, Allie," I said. "You needed that money. You needed it badly, because you were desperate to send Kenny to college out of state, away from this whole mess and, particularly, away from Laura before he found out that any relationship with her would be against the law in all fifty states. Kenny's going into his senior year, so he has to start applying to colleges soon, and that means filling out all those financial aid forms. You had to be able to show where the money was going to come from, because that's all the colleges are really interested in, especially those expensive, out-of-state schools, and they are *very* interested. So I'm betting that you told David that you'd have to tell Doreen about all of this if you didn't get the money. And once Doreen knew, the cat would be out of the bag one way or another, and he wouldn't be David Chandler, Mr. Squeaky Clean Local Hero anymore. People would still want to meet him at the bank, but for all the wrong reasons. Right, David?"

"Matt, you've got this all wrong," said David.

"No, I don't. And then what would you be? All you've ever been all your life is what you were in high school. You've got nothing else. Yeah, you've been in love with Allie since high school, and you wanted to do right by Kenny Junior, but only so long as David Chandler, Hometown Hero, was protected, because that's all you are. So you took your chances and borrowed the money from crooks, figuring that you'd worry about the repayment later. Something or someone would come along to bail you out, because that's how everything always worked for David Chandler. You were just desperate to buy time."

"I was just trying to do the right thing, dammit!"

"But," said Kenny, staring calmly at his father.

"But what?" said David.

"But you're ashamed of me. As long as you could keep everything a secret you were glad to help out. But you'll never acknowledge me publicly, will you?"

"You have to understand how complicated this whole thing is, Kenneth. I love you, you're my son, and you mean as much to me as my other children. I mean, look what I've done for you. But I have my reputation to think about. My standing in the community."

"You son of a bitch," came a quiet voice. It was Doreen. Her face was white, but her voice was calm.

David looked at her, but said nothing.

"You son of a bitch," said Doreen again. "No wonder you came home from college every weekend. You were coming to see Allie while I was away, weren't you?"

"Doreen, I…"

"You what, you son of a bitch? You married me because it fit the image that you wanted for yourself. In a really perverse way, I almost understand that. I remember the pressure on us; I remember the expectations. But you know what I don't get?" said Doreen, turning to face Allison Cooper. "What I don't get is you, Allie. How could you have let yourself be treated like that? My God, how could you have ever done that to your husband? What did he ever do to you to deserve that kind of betrayal?"

"That's all easy for you to say, isn't it, Princess Doreen of Devon?" replied Allie, almost snarling. "Look at you. You had everything. You had the brains, you had the looks, you had the popularity. You had everything, and I had nothing. You were the cheerleading captain; I was the last girl picked. You were the valedictorian of your class; I graduated in the bottom half of mine. You were the prom queen, while I went with Kenny, who ignored me all night and then got sick in the back of the car from drinking two six-packs beer with his buddies out on the football field. You went off to a fancy college and I stayed home and took a job with the phone company. And you had David." Her snarl turned into a sneer. "But, oh, you didn't have David, did you? The joke was on you, wasn't it, your highness?

Because David wanted me, *me*, not you. And David loved *me*, not you. And that made everything worth it."

"But what good did it do you, Allie?" I said. "David married Doreen, not you. And even after you had his baby, he stayed with Doreen, not you."

"David always told me that he had a plan, that what he was doing was for the best for us. He said once he established himself in his job and in the community, there would come a time when he could quietly divorce Doreen and we could have our life together."

"But that never happened," I said, "did it."

"I could be patient," said Allie. "I had Kenny Junior, and I knew David would never betray the two of us. And now the time has come, hasn't it, thanks to you, Matt, and Princess Doreen, getting caught with your pants down. Jesus, it just makes me want to laugh. Now David will be *my* husband, and *I'll* have the big house, and *I'll* have the big bank account. And now my son can know who his true father is, not that loser Kenny, and…"

"Allie," said David, cutting her off, "let's slow down here."

"What do you mean?" said Allie, turning to David, suddenly looking stunned.

"I mean, we have to be careful for a while longer, that's all."

"What do you mean, 'careful'? I thought you said we could get married right away now, as soon as your divorce was final."

"And we will, we will, I promise."

"Then what do you mean?" said Allie, but I could see by the look on her face that she starting to figure it out for herself.

"Look," said David, giving Kenny Junior a furtive look, "now's probably not the right time to talk about it."

"I don't understand, David," said Allie, almost whispering.

"Allie, please," said David, "just not now."

"No, David, now," said Allie, her voice becoming a growl.

"Look, Allie," said David, starting to look like a trapped animal, "I just think we have to be careful about acknowledging Kenneth Junior as my son."

"*What?*"

"Allie, please, calm down," said David. "Isn't it clear? We have the perfect justification for divorcing our spouses and marrying each other and keeping my reputation intact. These two," said David, waving his hand in the direction of Doreen and me, "gave us the perfect justification. But acknowledging Kenneth would make that all, you know, problematic. It ruins the entire scenario, don't you see?"

"But David," said Allie, "he's not a 'scenario', he's your *son*."

"I know that, Allie, but…"

"So, if you're not going to acknowledge him now, if now's not the right time, when will the right time be, David?"

"I just think that's something we're going to have to manage in the future, Allie. Once you give it some thought I'm sure you'll understand."

Allie suddenly stood up. It was her turn now.

"You son of a bitch."

"God, Allie, please…"

"You're never going to acknowledge him, are you?"

"I didn't exactly say that, Allie."

Allie didn't reply right away. She was making up her mind. She was making a decision. It didn't take her long.

"David, I want you to leave," she said when she finally spoke. "Now, David."

"What? Why?"

"Now, David."

"But, Allie. We can finally have what we've wanted for all these years! We can be together, and no one will ever be able to accuse us of doing anything wrong."

"As long as you never have to acknowledge me as your son, right *Dad*?" said Kenny Junior.

"Do you really think that's what's going to happen, David?" said Doreen, like she was talking to a stubborn child. "Do you really think that I'm just going to sit back and let you humiliate me and our children just so your precious reputation can be protected?"

"And do you really think I'm going to let you do that to our *son*?" said Allie.

"Look," he said, "can't we all sit down and talk about this like adults?"

"Oh, David," said Doreen, "that's so sad."

"What do you mean?" said David.

"You passed on your chance to be an adult a long time ago, David. I mean, look at you. You actually believe that the paltry little salary you earn at the bank to perform your dog and pony show whenever they tell you to actually pays our bills, don't you."

"David, what's she talking about?" said Allie, her eyes widening.

"I have no idea," said David, looking equally astonished.

"That's the pathetic thing," said Doreen, turning to Allie. "He actually doesn't know what he really is. So I'll tell you: David's just a third rate gofer at the bank, that's all, Allie. All that money he gave you over all those years? That was my money. I earned it. David makes less money at the bank than Kenny makes as Athletic Director. What, you thought you were going to run off with a rich banker? Is that what he's been telling you?"

"Doreen, you're going to have to explain all this to me," said David, his expression turning baffled.

"Don't worry, David," said Doreen, "you'll have it all explained to you during the divorce proceedings."

Allie turned to David, her face ashen but her voice calm.

"I don't understand any of this money talk, but right now, I'm not sure any of that matters. I would've stuck with you, David, no matter how the money stuff works out. I can get a job. I've lived modestly all my life, and I can keep doing that. But how can you betray your own son? That's what I can't ever forgive. Please, leave. I never want to see you again."

And David Chandler, my childhood friend, my teammate, stood up and walked out of the house without uttering a word, and without making eye contact with anyone. He didn't look back.

******

"Mr. Hunter?" said Kenny Junior. He was pale, but he was holding it together.

"Yes, Kenny?" I said. Doreen looked like she'd just tripped over a corpse, and I badly wanted to get her out of there; but I wasn't going to leave Kenny until I was sure he was okay. Allie looked like she'd withdrawn into a catatonic state, and I didn't think she'd be any help.

"I told you how I figured it out. Now I want to know how *you* figured it out."

"I guess I do, too," said Doreen, her voice surprisingly steady. Allie didn't react at all.

"I guess it was a few things that finally came together," I said. "I remembered running those routes with you, and when I thought back on it, I realized how much it reminded me of running routes with David."

"You mean, how my arm was so strong?"

"Yes, there was that, but it was more. It was your footwork; the way you moved, the way you cocked your head when you threw. It was all pure David. And then I remembered how your Dad told me that you'd suddenly quit football last year. That was about the time you found out, right?"

Kenny nodded. "Yeah, it was."

"But the oddest thing was when we talked at McDonald's that day, and you were so accepting of your Mom's rule that you couldn't date Laura Chandler. I mean, I was a teenager once, too, Kenny. When you've got the hots for a girl, you don't let much get in your way, you know? Especially not parental rules."

"Except when you've just found out the girl is your half-sister," said Kenny.

"Oh, God, Kenny," said Doreen, "I'm so sorry."

"It wasn't your fault, Mrs. Chandler," said the most mature kid I'd ever met. "I'm sorry this had to happen to you, too."

"But Matt," said Doreen, "I still don't understand what Lacey was talking about. How did she figure all this out?"

"That bugged me for a long time, too. But then I went back over the conversation we'd had. We'd talked a lot about how much David's reputation mattered to him, and how much he cared for his kids, and we just couldn't figure out what would drive him to disappear on them, and do something as stupid as borrow money from mobsters."

Doreen's eyes widened in recognition. "Another child," she said.

"And another woman he was in love with, obsessed with is more like it, for all these years. Suddenly, all the pieces fell in place for me. I'm just sorry it took me so long."

"Well, at least he did that," said Kenny.

"Kenny," I said, "I know you're probably not ready to hear this yet, but David Chandler is not as bad a man as he's made himself look today."

"I don't know about that," said Kenny. "All I know is that he might be my biological father, but he's not my Dad. I already have a Dad. I don't need another one. And Mom?"

Allie looked up. Her eyes were glazed, but I knew she'd listen to her son.

"Yes?"

"I don't want Dad to know about any of this. I don't know what you're going to do, but you have to do it without letting him know the real reason why. It would kill him."

"Don't worry, Kenny. I'm never going to speak to David Chandler again," said Allie, her eyes spilling over with tears. "Oh, God, Kenny, I'm so sorry."

"Maybe we can all try harder, you know?"

"Maybe we can," she said, her eyes lightening. "Maybe we can."

I rose to leave, and so did Doreen.

"I think it's time for us to get out of your hair," I said. Kenny walked over to me and held out his hand.

"Thanks, Mr. Hunter," he said. "I've been living with this by myself for way too long."

"I'm glad I could help," I said. I pulled him to me and gave him a hug. "I'll be around, okay?"

Kenny nodded, then went and sat down with his mother.

Doreen and I quietly slipped out the door.

CHAPTER THIRTY-FOUR

'LL BE LIVING IN THE DUPLEX FOR A WHILE.

Doreen and David are already divorced, but we don't think the kids need to see another man in the house right away. They've got another year in high school before they head off to college, and they don't need that kind of distraction. Doreen and I are still young. There's time.

David behaved as I'd hoped he wouldn't. When he found out just how much Doreen was worth during the divorce proceedings, he immediately tried to claim half. But Doreen let him know that there was a price for her silence. She offered him a million bucks, and he took it. He also lost his job at the bank shortly after the divorce. It had nothing to do with anything, I found out from Lacey, who knows everything. The bank just decided that nobody was really impressed with an aging high school football star anymore; and since he had no actual banking talents, they had no reason to keep him. From what I've heard, he's now selling overpriced term life insurance to retirees in Poughkeepsie. Who knows? Maybe he's found his calling.

The one who surprised me was Kenny, Senior.

I'd gone up to the Latitude Pub a few weeks after the big confrontation and ordered a Jupiler and stuffed baked potato skins without being prompted.

"My man," said Richie Glazier, beaming his approval. He must have seen me looking around the place, because he said, "If you're looking for Kenny, you're not going to find him here."

"What, has he finally moved on to other haunts?"

"Nah. From what I can tell, he's not going out at all anymore. Maybe the cooking's improved at home, if you know what I mean."

"I'm glad to hear that," I said.

"I hear the cooking's not so bad at your place these days, either."

"Not bad at all,"

"Not even my stuffed baked potato skins can compete with that cooking."

"No," I said, polishing off my last bite, "but they're a damn fine runner-up."

We'd both laughed, and I shook his hand before I left. Richie Glazier is good people.

A few weeks later I'd driven up to the high school on a whim. Kenny's office door was open, and he was sitting at his desk. He looked great. He looked like he'd lost about twenty pounds; his face was tanned, and it had lost a lot of the bloat.

The first thing I noticed besides Kenny's appearance was that the giant reproduction of The Picture was no longer on the wall.

"So, Kenny, I see you decided to change the décor."

"I thought it was time to move on, Matt."

"I couldn't agree with you more," I said. "You're looking great, Kenny. It looks like you could suit up again."

"I'm getting there. I made it a mile around the track this morning without stopping, and I didn't even have to puke when I was done."

"That's fantastic. I hope you can keep it up."

"Oh, I will. And Matt?"

"Yeah, Kenny?"

"I know. I know everything."

"Jesus, Kenny. How did you find out?"

"Aw, I guess I've known all along, but I just had a hard time admitting it to myself. Kenny Junior's my son, you know? I've loved him since the second I saw him, and nothing can change that. Genetics is one thing; being a Dad is another."

"No argument there," I said, thinking of my own kids, who I was visiting every weekend, despite the fact that a chinless orthodontist from Beacon was now occupying my side of Marianne's bed. I hadn't been impressed, and I guessed Marianne would have him out on the curb with the rest of the recycling before long. "So how did you actually find out for sure?"

"You know, after David left town things started to get better between Allie and me. She started asking me to stay home at night, and the three of us starting having our dinners together. It was nice. And she actually started, you know, to be interested in, you know, stuff."

"You always had a way with words, Kenny."

"So, anyway, one night we were lying in bed together, and I just blurted it out. I said, 'Allie, I think it's time we talked.' And we did."

"Does Kenny Junior know?"

"Yeah, he does. Is he a great kid or what?"

"He's an amazing kid, Kenny. You should be proud of him, and you should be proud of yourself. You raised a fine son."

"I don't know how good a father I've been, Matt, but I'm trying as hard as I can to change all that."

"So, I don't mean to be nosey, but how about you and Allie?"

"I don't know, Matt. There's a lot of hurt between us, but we're going to try. We're going to stick it out until Kenny Junior goes off to college, and then we'll see where we stand."

"I wish you the best, Kenny. Let's not be strangers, okay?" I said, as I rose to leave.

"Sounds like a plan."

"And Kenny?"

"Yeah?"

"I don't miss that damn picture. Not one bit."

"Neither do I, Matt. Neither do I."

******

The other big event was, of course, my sister's marriage.

Anthony Fornaio had looked almost handsome in a dark suit, although the aroma of rising dough still clung to him. He couldn't stop smiling. Lacey had bowed to the occasion and worn a dress. It was simple design made of unbleached cotton that Doreen had helped her pick out at a second-hand store, but it was a dress.

It had been a tiny affair, but Kenny and Allie had come, and they looked comfortable with each other.

Tommassino Fornaio had also attended along with his stunning wife, Christina. The reception was held in Anthony's tiny pizzeria behind his restaurant, and as I was diving into my second slice, Tommy took me aside.

"Matt," he'd said, "I'd like to congratulate you on a fine job."

"Thank you, Sir."

"Aw, c'mon, Matt. It's Tommy, okay? We're family now."

That kind of sent a chill up my spine, but I managed a smile and said, "Thanks, Tommy."

"It felt good, right?" he said.

"It felt better than anything's felt in a long time, Tommy."

"And now you have a beautiful woman in your life."

"Beautiful in more ways than I can think of," I said, "and I owe it to you."

"You did it yourself Matt," said my friend, the thug, looking at me with those piercing blue eyes of his. "Don't ever forget that."

"I won't," I said.

"And Matt?"

"Yes, Tommy?"

"You can stop worrying about that unfortunate business at the Halfmoon Diner. I'm on excellent terms with the local law enforcement authorities, and the owner of the diner is an old friend of mine. You're welcome in Halfmoon, and the diner, anytime."

"Thank you, Tommy," I said, meaning it. I'd been waiting for the second shoe to fall on that incident since the day it happened, and I was relieved to know that I could stop worrying. I wanted to know if Boiko had at least survived, but I knew well enough not to ask. I'd give Lieutenant Hudson a call and find out at some point. I thought briefly of liver and onions, and cherry pie.

We shook hands, and Tommy went back to rejoin his dazzling wife, leaving me alone, but not alone.

I was home now. I looked around the room. This was where I wanted to live out my life, and these were the people I wanted to spend it with. I'd wandered far, and I'd taken the long way back, but I'd finally made it.

My eyes came to rest on Doreen, the woman I'd loved long before I understood what love was. She was chatting happily with Lacey, and she gave me one of her patented smiles when she saw me looking at her. She had dressed simply, not to outshine the bride.

But, oh my, she looked good.

THE END

Made in the USA
Columbia, SC
11 February 2022

56022289R00129